Happy Holidate

SunflowerROSE
PUBLISHING

LAUREN W. ROACH

Author

Standalones

The Memory Concierge

Series

A Novel-Tea Christmas (1-5)

Socials

sunflowerrosepublishing.com

- thebookybabe
- thebookybabe_
- thebookybabe_
- thebookybabe
- thebookybabe
- LaurenRWrites
- buymeacoffee/thebookybabe

Hey bestie

Thank you so much for supporting my stories and believing in my work. Every read, review, and recommendation means more to me than I can put into words. Wouldn't be here without you.

If you'd like to stay connected, join my mailing list on my website (sunflowerrosepublishing.com) for updates, exclusive content, and special announcements.

You can also find bookish T-shirts and autographed copies of all my books there. I'm so grateful to have you on this journey with me.

Love Always,

Lauren

For the hearts that never stopped believing in Christmas magic

1

Deja

"As a high-value man, women should feel grateful to be in my presence," my date said. I shifted uncomfortably in my seat and tried to keep my face neutral. I was attempting to be positive. Even though I could tell this date was headed nowhere fast, I wanted to at least make it through the meal, so I could block him on my way out to the car. I was so thankful I decided to drive myself and meet him here. Being stuck with this guy, who spoke about women as if they were a possession to be owned, was a punishment I wouldn't wish on my worst enemy. "So, Darla, what did you say you do again?" he asked. I ignored the fact that he got my name wrong.

"I run my own marketing firm." I hated mentioning my job on dates. Whenever it came up in conversation, I would always try to dance around the question in the hopes that I could avoid answering. It never failed. Their eyes would immediately glaze over, or they would make a face. It was the type of career that automatically sounded like you were bragging about it, even if you were simply answering their question. Like clockwork, this guy recoiled almost as if he had been slapped.

"So, that means you're one of those high-maintenance types?" he asked. I couldn't even stop the heavy sigh that escaped my lips.

Another Flirtle date down the drain. It was a dating app one of my clients had created and was trying to launch. He'd hired me to help with the marketing and get the name circulating in the public, but so far, every date I'd gone on using his 'perfect match making criteria' had been a complete bust. This guy, I think he said his name was Caleb, looked at me expectantly. I'm assuming he wanted me to defend my case. I was supposed to laugh flirtatiously and assure him that I could be the brainless, spineless bird he desired me to be. Irritating. I didn't even bother to respond this time. Instead, I grabbed my purse and stood up from the table. "You have a good night, Caleb."

"It's Corey!" he called after me as I turned and left the restaurant. It's a shame I couldn't at least make it through dinner. It had been hours since I'd last eaten and this place was known for their macaroni and cheese, plus I wasted an outfit. I glanced down at my black turtleneck minidress and leather corset vest and sighed. I'd been so excited to channel my inner Regine Hunter with this vintage style outfit, and it was wasted on a loser that referred to himself as a 'high-value man'.

I grabbed my phone from my purse and called my friend Brina. She answered on the third ring.

"Either it was so successful that you've already seen him naked, or you left the date early." There was a hint of amusement in her voice. She already knew exactly why I was calling, my silence only confirmed it. "What was wrong with this one?"

"He asked if I was the high-maintenance type because I own a marketing firm." My response was met with silence. I flopped down into the driver's seat of my car and turned it on. I heard the familiar 'bloop' of my phone connecting to the car Bluetooth as soon as I turned the key. Brina's voice surrounded me as I pulled out of the parking lot. The famous macaroni and cheese would have to wait another day.

"That's *it*? Deja, you *are* the high maintenance type!" Her laughter reverberated through the car. The raspy tone of it much more obvious in the car speakers. I rolled my eyes. I wasn't high maintenance. I just had certain expectations that needed to be met before I considered someone a match. I had a reputation to uphold and an image I needed to protect. I couldn't have just anyone hanging around in my space, sucking up my air. "You turned down the last guy because you didn't like the way he smelled," she continued. I shuddered at the memory. He had reached for a hug and the smell that bounced off of his skin and his clothes made me want to lean over and gag.

"He smelled like green beans and hour seventy-four of a seventy-two-hour deodorant!"

"You expect perfection from these guys, Dej."

"Expecting someone to take a shower before a date is hardly expecting perfection," I retorted. "The first date is when you're on your best behavior. So, if you're falling short already then what is the point in continuing?"

Brina laughed again, "Fair point."

"We all can't dust off our childhood bestie and turn them into a Hallmark love story." I fought back my own smile as I pulled on to the highway to head back to my apartment. Brina and her boyfriend Langston had been best friends growing up before life sent them on different paths. Our friend group watched with heart eyes while he swooped in and made her his not long after they reconnected.

"True, but you know Elodie's wedding is in a few weeks, and she wants us all to have dates."

"Thank you for the painful reminder that I'm the last single one of the group." I grumbled. "I'm doing the best I can, but there isn't much to work with here."

"It doesn't have to be your forever match, just someone you can tolerate long enough to get through this wedding. Besides, isn't it your turn with the journal?"

I rolled my eyes. Technically, it was my turn with the journal we'd been passing through our five person friend group. It was the journal that'd led each of my girls to their perfect match. Even Monae, my girl who was so career focused as a firefighter, it took Jai almost burning down the kitchen for her to notice him.

I was excited to see who the journal would tell me to hookup with, but I didn't want to seem like I was desperate for a date. I'm fine on my own. I make good money and have plenty of dick on rotation if I have a specific itch that needs to be scratched, but I did crave the companionship. Sometimes. Then men like Corey pop up to remind me that maybe I am better off single. It's less of a headache.

"Well, the journal has a lot of work to do. I won't be matched with just any regular-degular man."

"Yes, Deja." Brina giggled, "I'm sure the journal has your laundry list of requirements in mind. You coming to brunch tomorrow?"

"Of course. I take my bridesmaid duties very seriously."

I pulled into my driveway and tried not to let my voice betray my feelings as I surveyed the scene in front of me. There on my porch stood my mother, with her arms folded, tapping her foot impatiently. I resisted the urge to put the car in reverse and speed out of the neighborhood.

"Let me call you back, babes. My mom is here." Before Brina could respond, I tapped to end the call and plastered on my best smile. "Hi, mommy. What are you doing here?"

"I called you twice and texted you three times. Since you didn't bother to respond to your poor mother, I figured I would come see what the issue was. Where were you?"

"I'm doing well, thanks. Would you like to come in?" I ignored her demand to know where I was and stepped around her to unlock the door. Adobe, my newly trained puppy, came bounding towards me as soon as I crossed the threshold. "Hi, baby!" I cooed, scooping his wiggly body into my arms.

"Honestly, Deja, that dress you're wearing is way too short. Where were you? I know you didn't go to work dressed like that."

"I was on a date. If you absolutely have to know," I replied over my shoulder.

"A date? How'd it go?"

"Not well."

"Well, maybe if you'd cover up your tattoos and put on a dress that didn't show so much skin, it'd be easier to find someone respectable. You cannot dress like a hooker and get mad when you are treated like one."

My back stiffened as the earlier confidence in my outfit drained from my body entirely. My mother, stout Christian woman that she was, held a lot of outdated views and opinions about me. Even though my dress came to my mid-thigh, and covered the rest of me, in her eyes I was half naked. As the head usher and decade long choir member, if the dress didn't come down to your ankles, you were doing too much. With her working as a wedding coordinator, you'd think she'd be used to seeing people with different mindsets and values, but that never translated to me. When it came to me, Denise Johnson expected her version of perfection.

"Why do you assume it's my fault?" I asked, trying hard to tamper the irritation. "Why couldn't he just have been a jerk? Why do you automatically contribute the failure to the way I look or dress?"

"Oh, Deja, must you be so *dramatic*? I am just trying to help you!"

"Okay, ma." There was no use fighting her on the situation. This was an ongoing battle that I had been trying to fight since I was fifteen and began to realize that she and I didn't like the same things. Sometimes it was easier to just let her think she won.

"So, Elodie's wedding is next month, do you have your dress?"

"I do." I leaned down to pour food into Adobe's bowl.

"And your date?"

"Still working on that."

"One of the ladies at the church has a son around your age. He's single. Good Christian man. I've given him your number." she sniffed, peeking into my refrigerator. "When are you going grocery shopping? Excessive takeout isn't good for-"

"Ma, I love you but if you just came over here to nitpick, then you really don't need to stay. I've got a long day at work tomorrow."

My day was relatively relaxed for tomorrow, but she didn't need to know that. As much as I loved my mother, sometimes she could be a handful to deal with. I'd already had enough on my plate with Elodie's rapidly approaching wedding and a few client campaigns launching around the same time. The last thing I needed was her voice in my head, making me second guess my decisions.

"Don't be so sensitive about what I'm telling you. I'll leave. I know you're busy." My mother leaned forward and planted a kiss on my cheek, "I just worry about you sometimes. Answer the phone when I call, so you don't stress your poor mother."

I rolled my eyes but smiled, "Yes Ma'am."

"Hey, ladies!" I gushed, waving at my friends. I was the last one to arrive at our usual brunch spot. All four of my friends: Brina, Elodie, Audrey, and Monae were sitting at the table sipping mimosas when I arrived twenty minutes late.

"Your mom is fabulous!" Elodie grinned, before I even sat down. "Thank you so much for recommending her for our wedding. Those last two coordinators I met with were trash."

My girls were not familiar with the dynamic between my mother and I, making it difficult to explain why her increased presence during this process would be added stress for me. As much as I hated to admit it, my mother was the best in the game and I wanted the best for my girl. I could suck it up for the time being.

"Only the best for you, my love." I winked at her and pulled out the menu. "What did you guys order? Are we leaning more towards drinks or food this time?"

"Food, I'm meeting Jai later so we can strategize about the Christmas event this year." Monae smiled down at her phone as she talked. She rarely got days off with her hectic work schedule, but when she did, every free moment was spent with Jai. I loved seeing him thaw her out last year while their love story developed. Monae was always the quieter one out of the group, choosing to observe more than she spoke. Jai, with his gentle, fun-loving demeanor, pulled her out of her shell and opened up a new side of her none of us had seen before.

"Make sure wherever you go has a room you two can sneak off to when the mood hits." I wiggled my eyebrows playfully.

Monae's head snapped up, eyes widening in embarrassment. "Deja!"

"I'm just saying!" I laughed, "You took care of business in more ways than one."

"Speaking of that." She snapped her fingers and then reached into the bag that was sitting next to her foot, "You know the drill."

My heart thudded in my chest as she placed the leatherbound journal, that was quickly becoming a staple in our friend group, on the table in front of me. Conversation grew quiet as we all stared. To most, it was an old book that looked like it had seen better days, but to us, it was turning out to be so much more than that. I'd watched the last few years as it directed Elodie towards Mekhi, Audrey to Montrell, Brina to Langston, and then Monae to Jai.

I waited patiently, hoping each time that my turn would be next. Instead, it picked everyone but me, while I faithfully talked my girls through their emotions and listened as they freaked out about taking the plunge into the relationship they had always wanted. I approached each situation like I would have with one of my clients who was just starting their new brand or business and needed help wading through the scary parts.

I'd done it four times, each time wondering when it would be my turn. I looked down at the journal, almost scared to touch it. What if it made me wait this long just to tell me that my match wasn't out there? What if it said I was doomed to match with losers on Flirtle until I grew old and died alone?

"Saved the best for last." I giggled, with an air of confidence, I did not feel. A small tingle hit my fingertips as soon as they connected with the journal. Almost as if it was telling me that it could hear me. "This thing has a lot of work to do."

"I'm excited to see who it tells you your match is." Brina grinned. "I am excited to see if this unicorn exists."

"As long as the unicorn dick is in his pants and not on his

forehead." I shrugged.

The table erupted in giggles at my foolishness. I sighed inwardly, happy to have redirected the conversation. I was worried the longer we talked about this journal, the more my interest in finding a match would begin to read as desperation and that was the last thing I wanted.

The rest of the brunch was smooth sailing. I offered feedback on the last-minute wedding details, gushed at the pictures everybody showed from when they were trying on their bridesmaids dresses, and gave my opinion on which book we should focus on for book club.

My phone vibrated in my pocket midway through the meal, with a text from my mom. I knew whatever it was would put a damper in my mood and I didn't want to ruin the fun. Getting together with my girls was always the highlight of my day. Being able to let my hair down and relax with the four women who have seen me at my best and at my worst, over the years, gave me the energy to get through meetings with tough clients.

I waited until we had all hugged goodbye and gone our separate ways to glance down at my phone. I had a coffee in my other hand to help me power through the rest of the day.

Make sure your clothes are presentable. People talk and you want their first impression of you to be the best! A nice pantsuit would probably do the trick. Don't forget to iron! Love you!

I stared at the words, using my strength to fight back the

irritation. I know she meant well, she always does, but it still managed to get under my skin. So much so, that I'd stopped paying attention to where I was walking. I vaguely heard the horns and the screeching tires before my brain could register what was even happening. I felt myself being yanked backwards just as an eighteen-wheeler sped by, blaring its horn angrily.

The coffee I'd been holding splattered down the front of my dress and I fell to the ground with an, "oof!" Something firm had broken my fall. I hurried to my feet, dazed and glanced down at my dress, now covered in the light brown coffee.

"Crap." I muttered. "I needed that."

"Yo, you good?" a deep voice rumbled from behind me. I turned, finally realizing what, or rather, who, had broken my fall.

He was the kind of man who made the air feel heavier when he stepped close, like his presence alone rearranged the atmosphere. His locs fell in long, thick ropes over his shoulders, a rich cascade of dark and sun-kissed strands that framed a chocolate brown face both striking and unreadable. His jawline was sharp enough to carve through stone, softened only by the neatly kept beard that gave him an effortlessly regal look.

His eyes held a quiet intensity, the sort that made me feel like I was being examined under a microscope in a way I wasn't prepared for. He had a calm confidence about him, the kind that didn't need to announce itself. Broad shoulders filled out his shirt, and even relaxed, he carried himself like a man who understood his own strength.

It took me a second to realize who he was. I was so thrown off by this being the first time I saw him in person, that my mind completely blanked for a second. Rashaad Clairfield, the COO and right hand to Langston, my friend Brina's boyfriend. Langston and Rashaad ran Brain Box, one of the most successful toy building companies in the United States. He had reached out to me for some marketing help as they wished to expand into multiple locations.

"Rashaad, right?" I flashed him a grin full of confidence, even though I stood in front of him wearing my coffee. His eyebrow raised as he silently took me in. "Deja. Brina's friend. We spoke about a possible rebrand."

"Deja Johnson? Oh wow, I didn't expect to run into you." He grasped my hand in his and gave it a firm shake. "Luckily for you, one of us was paying attention."

I laughed. "Not my proudest moment. I'd seen a text from my mom and-" I sighed and trailed off, embarrassed that I'd divulged that much information right off the bat. Something flickered in his expression, something that looked like understanding.

"Bad news?"

"No, not at all. Just-" I waved my hand dismissively and he nodded.

"I get it. Hey, at least let me buy you another coffee."

As we walked back in the direction of the coffee shop, I pushed my mother's words out of my mind. It was a beautiful day out and even though my off-white sweater dress was stained with coffee, I still looked good. I had an extra outfit in the office I could change into when I arrived, so I wasn't worried about it.

I gave my order to the barista and turned to Rashaad. I had

been right. When I heard him in Brina's office a while ago when she was working with Brain Box on getting a copyright issue settled. He sounded attractive over the phone and seeing him now with the tattoos peeking out from under the sleeve of his shirt confirmed it.

"So how long have you been in marketing?" he asked.

"I started my own firm a few years out of school and have been grinding ever since," I replied, flashing a smile at the barista who handed me my coffee.

"I've been following your track record. You've done some really dope work. Your name has been on a lot of branding campaigns."

I turned to him, surprised. "You've been following my work?"

"Absolutely. I do my research before agreeing to get into bed with someone."

"Oh?" I raised an eyebrow and took a sip of my coffee; the warm liquid had the perfect amount of cinnamon and caramel. I resisted the urge to close my eyes. "Well, did you like what you saw?"

Rashaad studied me for a minute while I waited for his answer. I watched as his eyes took in every inch of me and if I'm honest with myself, I was enjoying it more than I expected. "I did."

My buzzing phone snatched my attention before I could offer a cheeky response. It was my client with the dating app, excited to know how my experience had been with it. I bit my lip, not wanting to ruin his mood by telling him the criteria he used to match me with Corey needed work.

"I look forward to working with you, Mr. Clairfield. Reach out to my office when you're ready to get started."

"You'll be hearing from me soon, Ms. Johnson," he replied, a hint of a smirk on his lips. I tipped my coffee in his direction and turned on my heels. As attractive as he was, I needed to get to work. Between bridesmaid's events and a few clients wanting to launch new products in time for Black Friday and Christmas, I had a lot of work to catch up on.

The app is clean, but the criteria needs tweaking.

I sent the message and then quickly put my phone back in my purse. I narrowly escaped an accident less than an hour ago, I didn't want to push my luck again this soon. By the time I'd made it into my office, my mind was buzzing with new ideas for the Flirtle app. He wanted this to be up and running by January so we could have a solid launch season for Valentine's Day.

I'd just sat down at my desk to work on the photoshoot vibe for my client with her new lip gloss line, when my purse toppled over on my desk. The corner of the journal peeked out, and I excitedly reached for it, hoping there was a message for me. Just a few words that could offer me an ounce of clarity would be perfect.

But there was nothing.

Empty pages. No witty messages, no short passages directing me towards the love of my life. My heart sank. Did this mean there wasn't a match for me? I closed the journal and shoved it back into my purse.

I've made a few tweaks. Try again! I'm determined to get this right before the relaunch.

I shook my head but opened the app anyway. The app interface still looked the same for the most part, but I could see the subtle changes as I scrolled through. A red notification popped up in my messages while I was browsing. I hesitated, not wanting to ruin my decent mood by interacting with someone who could end up being a disappointment, but this was for research. Right? There was a match from a man named Xavier. A quick glance at his profile told me that he was a few years older than me, worked in the IT field, and spent a lot of time in the gym. Not bad, I guess.

Do you know what my shirt is made of?

I sighed, typing in a quick response.

Let me guess, boyfriend material?

The typing bubbles popped up immediately. I put my phone down on the desk and turned back to my computer, losing interest in the conversation. His opening line was so disappointing, I couldn't imagine him doing anything else to impress me, even if he was easy on the eyes.

"Hey, Dee?" I looked up at the sound of my assistant Jorja's voice. "Do you mind if I leave a little early today? My mom has been hounding me for weeks about taking her to the store so she can shop this sale and-"

"Absolutely." I smiled. Jorja was a godsend. When I was so deep in a brand or website launch that I forgot what day it was, she would always make sure I came up for air and remembered to eat. "Tell Ms. Elena I said hi and I'm looking forward to my slice of lemon cake."

Jorja rolled her eyes. "You are the only reason she even bothers to make it anymore. Whenever my brothers and I ask, she tells us to make it ourselves."

Elena Green made the best lemon cake in the state. Hands down. Audrey and Montrell, the two chefs of the group couldn't dispute the fact that a slice of her lemon cake was like no other. I had been begging for the recipe, but she refused to give it up. Elena knew she was sitting on a goldmine, but the idea of profiting from her talents never interested her. She cooked for love, not money and no matter how many creative ways I tried to come up with to coax her into it, she was not budging. I had to respect her stance, at the end of the day.

Jorja and her mom had the type of mother-daughter relationship I craved with my own mom. They were best friends—thick as thieves—and hung out constantly. Elena was warm, encouraging, and accepting in a way my mother never was. I found myself living through their stories and their moments, imagining that one day my mom and I could experience something similar. It was a long shot, but the little girl in me still hoped for it. Maybe one day.

Jorja promised to update me with the items her mom purchased at the sale and then headed back to her desk, allowing me time to focus on what I needed to get through. With Thanksgiving being in a few days, and Elodie's wedding being the week of Christmas, it felt like I had no real time to devote to my clients.

I glanced down at my phone as the notification sound chimed. Anthony had responded to my message.

That was painfully corny, I already know. That's my fault. Can I take you to dinner tonight to make it up to you?

His response did earn a small smile from me. If he at least understood that his opening line was corny, then maybe dinner couldn't hurt. I wasn't expecting my forever, I just needed someone I could tolerate long enough to work as my date for this wedding. The happily ever after could come later.

A gentle whishing sound from my purse made me freeze in my tracks. I'd gotten so caught up in my work that I'd forgotten about the journal. I pulled the journal out of my bag and placed it gingerly on my desk. It vibrated as if it had a notification and I watched in awe as the pages flipped back and forth on their own. I'd seen this process a few times in my friend group, and each time filled me with excitement. Maybe I was one step closer to finding my forever.

Dear Diary,

The hardest lesson Deja will have to learn is this: you cannot hide behind sparkles and expect to be truly seen.

The one meant for her will not be dazzled by her shine or fooled by her performance. He will notice the woman beneath the glitter, the one she guards so carefully, even from herself.

He'll see her in a moment she'd rather forget, when her light flickers and her confidence slips. A moment that feels small, unflattering, unbecoming of the woman she presents to the world. Yet, he will see her clearly and still choose her.
But only if she allows him to look past the reflection she's crafted, and into the truth she keeps tucked away.

"You can't hide behind sparkles and expect to be seen," I muttered and rolled my eyes at the journal as if it could hear me. "I'm not hiding. I'm literally trying to make your job easier."

If it had gently nudged my friends in the direction of their match, why couldn't I just help out by going on dates? It'd been a few years, maybe the journal was a little rusty. A quick dinner wouldn't hurt.

I glanced up at the clock and typed a quick response to Xavier, telling him I would meet him at the restaurant tonight at seven. That gave me plenty of time to wrap up things here and then go home and freshen up a little before the date. My coffee-stained sweater dress would have been the perfect dress to wear out tonight, stylish but not trying too hard, but I wouldn't have enough time to get the stain out.

He will see her clearly and still choose her. The words from the cryptic journal entry replayed in my head for the rest of the day. I couldn't pinpoint what it meant. What unflattering moment will this mystery man catch me in?

My thoughts continued to spiral in the background while I

closed out my work computer and gathered my things. I had no idea what to expect on this date, but the more I thought about it, the more excited I became. It sounded like this would be the beginning of something beautiful. I could only hope that it didn't hurt in the process.

2

Rashaad

I saw her and for a second, everything else in sight lost its edges. My racing thoughts slowed to a crawl, and it felt like the sky opened up around her. I found myself tracking her movements as she studied something on her phone. I kept waiting for her to look up, for her to catch my eye, but she didn't. Whatever was on her phone had her full concentration, her brow furrowed. The heavy afternoon traffic zipped dangerously by, getting closer and closer as she continued moving. She hadn't been paying attention to her surroundings and was quickly walking towards an intersection that was rushing with cars. If she didn't look up soon, this would easily turn from a refills day into a tragic situation.

My feet began to move, and before I could register what I was doing, I was racing up to her and yanking her backwards. Just as an eighteen-wheeler whirled past, blaring its angry horn. Her body was soft against mine as I pulled it into me. We fell to the ground in a clumsy heap of limps and coffee cups. The liquid splattered all over the front of her dress, as she hurried back to her feet, offering me the chance to really take her in while she was distracted with her dress.

Her features were striking in a way that crept up on me: warm, velvety skin that held a soft glow, and eyes that were deep and alert, framed by lashes that made her gaze feel even more intentional.

"Yo, you good?" I managed to choke out. When she finally looked up at me, it took every ounce of my self-control not to take her back into my arms. Her curls were a beautiful, textured halo, spiraling around her face as if each strand was determined to make its presence known. Her lips were soft, full, and lightly glossed, inviting without trying to be. She looked like someone who knew how to carry herself, someone impossible to overlook even if she never asked to be seen. She had curves for days and the sweater dress she wore highlighted every mouth-watering contour and arch from her hips to her shoulders.

I'd never seen a woman who could make a stained dress look like high fashion and I was in awe. I needed to know more about this girl.

"Rashaad, right?" She grinned at me. I tilted my head, confused. She knew me. How? As if sensing my question, she smiled even wider and stuck out her hand. "Deja. Brina's friend. We spoke about a possible rebrand."

"Deja Johnson? Oh wow, I didn't expect to run into you." I grasped her hand in mind, noting how soft her skin was. "At least one of us was paying attention."

She took my jab in stride and laughed. The sound hit my ears and sent a shock up my spine.

"Not my proudest moment. I was reading a text from my mom and-" Her expression faltered and the smile that was just there, slipped.

"Bad news?" I asked.

"Not, not at all, just-" she paused again and then waved her hand as if pushing the conversation away from her. I knew that feeling. I understood it deep in my soul, my mind drifted back to a conversation I'd had with my father a few days prior. It'd left me feeling hollow and heavy at the same time. Like it always did. Exactly like she looked right now.

"I get it." I didn't want her to feel pressured to explain anything to me that she wasn't comfortable with. "Hey, at least let me buy you another coffee."

I changed the subject, hoping to see that smile reappear. Knowing firsthand what complicated parental relationships felt like, and whenever my father and I weren't vibing well, the last thing I wanted was to discuss it with a stranger on the street.

She agreed and fell into step beside me as we headed back to the coffee shop.

That was all it took for Deja Johnson to occupy my thoughts for the rest of the day. I wanted to know her. Not only did her business sense impress me, she impressed me and it wasn't often that happened.

"Long day?" Langston, my best friend and business partner, entered my office and settled into the chair across from my desk.

I smirked, "Something like that."

He let out a loud yawn and then stretched. "Man, Brain has been keeping me up so late these days."

I glared at him, seeing his thinly veiled bragging for exactly what it was. Brain was the silly nickname he'd given his current girlfriend, Brina, when they were kids. He claimed that she had always been one of the smartest people he'd ever known. Even named his entire company after her.

"I'm elated on your behalf." I deadpanned.

"It's going to happen for you one day." He grinned, wiggling his eyebrows, "And I, for one, can't wait to meet the woman that brings you to your knees."

Deja's gentle smile flashed in my thoughts, but I blinked it away. "Such a woman does not exist. Anyway, I saw your email. We're meeting with investors tonight?"

"Yes." Langston sat up straighter, immediately snapping into business mode. "I've been trying to get on his schedule for months and he finally had an opening tonight. We're meeting him at Ember & Ivory tonight at seven."

As much as I would have preferred to head home early after work and rest, I'd be there helping Langston secure these investors. He knew without asking that I would rearrange my schedule to be there for him, because that's what I do. Usually, it was never a problem, but after our company took a crucial hit because his ex-girlfriend was leaking information to our competitors, he'd started to lean on me a little harder. I understood why. After being betrayed by one of the closest people to you, it gets hard to trust new people. Even if the situation did reconnect him with his childhood best friend and long time love interest, Langston was still extremely careful about who he confided in. There was no question where my loyalty stood, which meant there was no question who he expected to be around for everything.

"Alright. I've been meaning to try their Ribeye," I replied.

Langston stood and turned for the door, "Also, we have the wedding stuff coming up. Brina is one of the bridesmaids and the wedding party is doing a bunch of get togethers and events with the plus ones. I might be in and out until it's over."

"I can handle things while you're gone. You know this."

"My man. I've got a few things to take care of before I wrap up for the day. I'll see you at Ember & Ivory." He tapped on the doorframe with his knuckles as he left.

I took the next few hours of silence to catch up on my work, counting down the seconds and minutes until I could make it through dinner then home to finally relax.

People think that being the COO meant you were used to chaos. Incorrect. Chaos is loud, messy, and unpredictable. I do my best to avoid it in every aspect of my life, relationships included. Precision and purpose are what carried me to the finish line every single time. It's what my father drilled into my skull as soon as I could talk. *You must be controlled. You cannot be messy. School your emotions until you are in private.*

Langston likes to remind me that life can't always be controlled, which is hilarious coming from a man who planned an entire fairytale for a woman he's loved since his childhood days. He was allowed the privilege to let go and see what happened because he always had me in front to catch the fallout before it got to him. Langston was the creative one. He was the heart behind the operation and the passion behind the project. I was the brain. He threw the idea in my lap, and I made it happen. Not because I'm sentimental, but because I'm loyal and I've become a pro at shoving it all down until later.

So even though I was tired, and I wanted nothing more than to shed this suit so I could feel free for the night, I was here at this restaurant, ready to convince this investor that we were a good financial decision.

As soon as I opened the door to Ember & Ivory, I knew I'd made a mistake. Too many people. Too much perfume. Too many conversations all morphing together into one loud, indistinguishable murmur.

The place felt like old money that made the room hum with a quiet confidence. The lighting was warm and low, casting a soft amber glow over everything and giving it just enough gleam without trying too hard. Dark marble wrapped around the hostess stand and the center partition and the green velvet seating drew the room together. It was elegant, slightly stuffy, with an intentional minimalism that could only be achieved with commas on the price tag. Deals were struck in restaurants like this, where the atmosphere alone whispered that failure wasn't an option.

My father would love it here. As a businessman himself, he thrived in environments like this, where even the air smelled expensive. I followed the hostess to our table, taking in the rest of the view around me. The floor to ceiling windows revealed a balcony that overlooked the skyline.

I adjusted my suit jacket and squared my shoulders. I would do my part, get through this meeting and then head to The Kickback to get a milkshake and head home. No sweat. The waitress placed the menus on the table with a half-hearted smile. "I'm Mercedes. Have you gentlemen been here before?"

"I have." Langston grinned.

"My wife and I come here often." Draymond Bell, our potential investor, replied. This man was a legend in the black community. His family had come from incredibly humble beginnings but managed to build and connect and invest until they created something that would have the entire family set for generations to come.

"I guess I'm the newbie, then." I nodded at the waitress who lazily dragged her gaze across my face, "What do you recommend I try?"

"The Matsutake Mushrooms and the Wagyu beef are our most popular options," she deadpanned.

"Maybe another time. I'll try the Ribeye, though."

The waitress nodded, scribbling it down on the notepad before turning to Langston and Draymond to take their orders. While they spoke, I took the opportunity to look around the restaurant. My gaze caught on a couple by the table. The woman chatted animatedly while the man was quite obviously ogling her breasts.

Even from here, I could tell that he wasn't picking up on a word she said.

It took me a second, because of the distance, to register why she caught my eye. It was Deja. She was on what looked to be a date. She'd changed out of the dress I'd seen her in earlier into something that put her figure on display. And what a figure it was. The glittery dress hugged every curve from her breasts to where it stopped above her knees. Tattoos on full display and something about the way she talked, not caring if the guy was paying attention, made me want to pay attention.

I wanted to know what she was talking about. I wanted to be the one sitting across the table from her. I should look away, go back to the dinner so I could focus my attention on this meeting with Draymond and his company. I should. But I don't.

"What are you staring at?" Langston muttered with a sharp elbow to the ribs.

"I don't stare." I said flatly, "I was observing the decor in this place. What made you pick it, Mr. Bell?"

"Oh," he began, fully unaware of my attempt to save face. "My wife loves this place. It was a good excuse to bring her some takeout. Smooth things over. We aren't seeing eye to eye at the moment. You know how that is." He rolled his eyes, but there was a smile on his face.

"I know what you mean. My Brain, I mean Brina, drives me crazy often, but I wouldn't trade her for the world."

"Exactly." They both turned to me, waiting for me to contribute, but I had nothing to offer. My gaze, however, drifted back over to the table where Deja and her mystery date sat. I looked over just in time to see him reach across and touch her leg. She shifted in her seat and tried to remove his hand, but he tried again. She glanced around with a strained smile, while he tried his best to slip his hand up the hem of her dress.

Heat boiled underneath my skin the longer I watched. I wanted to grab his hand and bend back each finger one by one until he-

SMACK!

With her free hand, Deja had reached up and slapped him in the face. Her hand connected to his cheek with a loud crack, causing a few people to glance over in that direction.

The guy leaned back in his chair, clutching his cheek. "Stingy, broke, bi-" .

"I'd think really hard about the next words that leave your mouth," Deja hissed with a surprising amount of strength. I watched, as she stood up from the table, squared her shoulders, and then walked calmly out onto the balcony. But not before I saw the hurt in her eyes.

"Excuse me." I stood from the table.

"What? Where are you going?" Langston called, but I was already halfway through the restaurant.

"I need to check on something," I called over my shoulder, not breaking my stride. I'd catch hell for this later. Without turning to look at him, I already knew that Langston was flexing his jaw like he always did when he was angry. I'd deal with it later. Right now, I had a different focus.

The air outside was crisp as soon as I stepped out. The noise from the restaurant faded behind me, the silence welcoming. I scanned the balcony, looking for Deja. I spotted her in the corner, away from the view of the windows. Her shoulders were slumped in a moment of vulnerability. Part of me wanted to turn and head back into the restaurant so she could have her moment to herself, but the other part of me, the louder part, needed to check on her.

"You good?" I asked quietly, when I was within earshot.

She whirled around to face me, the hurt in her eyes morphing into surprise. "Rashaad? What are you doing here?"

"Checking on you."

Her shoulders fell, "How much of that did you see?"

"All of it," I replied, slipping off my jacket and placing it around her bare shoulders. "If you want, I could go punch him in the other cheek."

Her laugh was quiet, but it made her entire face light up. Something twisted in my chest at the sight. I smiled, leaning against the railing next to her. We were the only two on the balcony so far, everyone else was inside the restaurant enjoying their food.

"I met him off a dating app my client is working on. I wasn't even going to go, but everybody has been riding my ass about finding a date for this wedding, especially my mom."

"Why do you need a date?"

"She's the wedding coordinator, and according to her, it looks bad on her image if her own daughter can't find someone to escort her to the wedding. Since I'm one of the bridesmaids." She rolled her eyes.

"You don't have any male friends you could lean on just to keep up appearances?"

"None that haven't tried to shove their tongue down my throat at some point."

"You need better friends."

She snorted. "Thank you for coming out here to check on me. I'm fine, though. I don't want to keep you away from your date."

"It's a meeting with a potential investor," I corrected, for some reason, needing her to know that I wasn't on a date.

"Right. Well, I won't hold you."

I nodded, taking the not so sudden hint of dismissal in stride. She handed me my jacket, the earlier glimpse of vulnerability and sadness completely gone. I turned, making my way back to the door so she could have some privacy.

"I'm still waiting for your call," she said. I glanced back to see her looking in a small compact mirror, touching up her makeup. When I didn't respond, she snapped the mirror shut and winked at me. "Brain Box needs me if they want to expand appropriately. Investors bring the money, but the marketing brings the buzz."

"You'll hear from me soon."

I pulled the door open and headed back to my table, ready to do damage control.

"Where was your head during dinner?" Langston asked, folding his arms across his chest. We were standing in the parking lot debriefing after our meeting with Draymond Bell. Things had gone well after I came back to the table and truly locked into the conversation, but it did take a second for Mr. Bell to warm back up to us.

It ended on a positive note, but I know Langston had been dying to cuss me out after my initial behavior. Couldn't blame him for being concerned. It was unlike me to not be focused. Seeing Deja had momentarily paused everything for me.

I sighed, "I saw a guy getting real handsy with a girl and I wanted to go check on her to see if she was good. That's all."

Langston narrowed his eyes. "Since when do you take on the role of Knight in Shining Business Suit?"

"Relax. It's not that serious; she just seemed upset, and I wanted to check on her. We got what we needed. Bell Investments is open to partnering with us."

"There is potential for more though. I need you to find a date and come to this wedding."

"For your girlfriend's best friend? For what, nigga?" My irritation slipped out, but I didn't bother to catch it.

"Potential investors, nigga," Langston replied, matching my irritation word for word, bar for bar.

"For an English teacher and a music teacher?"

"You forget Elodie is now an author and Mekhi was a well-known musician before he started at the school. Plus, Audrey and Montrell will be there, and their restaurants have gotten huge since that cooking competition a few years ago. There will be some big names at this wedding."

"Why do I need to bring a date?"

Langston placed his hands on my shoulders. "You know how optics look during the holiday season. They look for warm, stable and family centered. Not the uninhibited playboy. We almost lost Draymond when you couldn't pitch in the simple conversation about a relationship."

I glared at him, wanting nothing more than to shrug his hands off my shoulders and leave him standing here in the parking lot looking lonely. We both knew I wouldn't do that. As crazy as he had been driving me lately, Langston was still my best friend. We both knew I would do whatever needed to be done.

"Where am I supposed to find a date?"

"I'm sure you can make something happen. You always do." He clapped me on the shoulder. I watched, annoyed, as he clicked his key fob and headed in the direction of the flashing lights. "You've got about a month to find a date."

"I guess."

"Maybe it'll end up being the woman that finally makes you loosen your tie a little."

"Fairytales are for children," I called after him. "I am a grown ass man. I just need a quick date."

"Whatever you say, Mr. Grown Ass Man." His laughter carried as he got in his car and closed the door behind him, leaving me in the parking lot by myself. I waited for him to pull out of the parking lot before I headed to my car.

My wheels had already started turning with an idea to solve everyone's problems quickly developing right before my eyes. I needed a date, but I needed someone that wasn't going to be up under me, expecting me to entertain them the majority of the night. The goal was to score investors and if I was to do so, I needed to be able to focus.

I had an idea that would potentially ease everyone's troubles. Just had to make sure everyone involved was completely onboard.

The next morning, instead of calling into the office like I promised I would, I got dressed and headed up to Deja's firm. The more I thought about it, the more the idea seemed like it could work, but that was only if she was on board as well.

I pushed through the glass doors before I could talk myself out of it and instantly felt like I'd walked into someone's imagination come to life. The first thing that hit me was the wall. It was an explosion of color that stretched across the far side of the room. A mural so bold it felt like the paint strokes had come alive and it was breathing. It felt like it would shift if I blinked too long. Reds, golds, blues, and flashes of neon colors all tangled together in a way that shouldn't make sense on paper, but it did in person. It was loud, unapologetic, and impossible to ignore.

Exactly like Deja.

Rows of desks lined the floor, each one decked out with bright white computers that stood out against the color behind them. The chairs were modern and quirky, shaped like something you'd find in an architectural or interior design museum. The entire space felt open and energetic. Sunlight poured in through the tall windows.

I could hear soft conversations from people sitting at the desks. The clicks of keyboards and the hum of ideas forming in real time. I tugged at my shirt, nerves getting the better of me momentarily. Business meetings were no sweat, but this wasn't just any type of business deal. This wasn't your regular proposition. I could have-no, I should have called, but something told me that my presence would matter more for something like this. Showing up in person said something that a phone call wouldn't.

"Can I help you?" A young woman asked, after noticing me standing there absorbing the energy of the room like fuel.

"Yes, I'm here to see Deja Johnson."

"Is she expecting you?" The woman glanced down at the iPad resting against her forearm. Her thick brows furrowed slightly as she ran down the list of meetings on the schedule looking for my name. She wasn't going to find it.

"No, but give her my name. She may be able to squeeze me in."

The woman shrugged and turned on her heels, clicking away down the hall. It only took a few minutes for her to come back, "Have a seat in the waiting area, she'll be right with you."

I took a seat near the window to wait for Deja, trying to figure out a gameplan for how to pitch this idea to her. It made so much sense at the house and in the car on the way here, but now that I was in her office, my nerves were starting to get the better of me.

"Mr. Clairfield." Her voice cut through the loud spiral of my thoughts and pulled me back to the present. "It's nice to see you again. For the third time...in two days."

"Same to you. Can we speak in your office?"

I followed behind her to a large private office in the back. The decor was nothing like the vibe in the front and while it was still colorful and fun, there was a gritty undertone to it. I looked around, noting the paintings on the walls and the skillfully placed photographs. It reminded me of Brina's office when I'd popped up at her firm to recruit her help a few years back, this was just the bolder version.

"Finally ready to take Brain Box higher than you could have ever imagined?"

"Yes, but maybe not in the way you had originally pitched." The plush chair in front of her desk nearly swallowed me up as I sank down into it. It felt like sitting on a cloud. I settled for a moment, allowing my body to relax. The only way I would get through this meeting is if I could unclench my jaw and unstiffen my shoulders.

"What do you mean?" Deja replied, sitting in her chair and crossing her legs. A piece of her Medusa thigh tattoo peeked out from under the knee length skirt she wore. I pulled my gaze away from her leg and focused on the bookshelf behind her, scanning the books for a title I possibly recognized.

"I have a proposition for you," I began, completely forgetting everything I'd rehearsed in my head. "It'll solve your problems and a problem I've recently acquired."

"Elaborate." Her gaze was wary, professional but not unwelcoming. Gone was the woman who was chatting animatedly at the restaurant, without a care or concern in the world. I briefly wondered if I'd be able to experience that version of her for myself.

"Let me be your date to this wedding."

Deja's head tilted in confusion, "What? Buying me coffee after bumping into me hardly seems like enough for all that."

I laughed. "That's fair, but not like that. Nothing romantic. Purely professional. You need a date to get your mother off your back. I need a date that won't be up under me so I can focus on getting near some potential investors. We both get what we want with no feelings involved."

"And your solution to my boring love life is a fake dating situation? Are we in a Hallmark movie?" She smirked, folding her arms. "Is this where we accidentally fall in love and then ride off into the sunset?"

"No, but I know you'd like to have a moment of peace and I'm happy to provide that in return for an invite to this wedding. It's no pressure, no expectations. You can focus on being the best bridesmaid you can be, and I'll help you keep your mother off your back."

She stared at me closely and then shook her head, as if warding off whatever thought crept into her mind. "As... persistent as my mother is, she's not the only one clocking my love life. I have four very intelligent, very nosey best friends that have all found their soulmates. They've been rooting for me to find my match from day one. They're going to grill the hell out of any date I bring."

"I can handle your friends."

"You say that now, but stronger people have cracked under the pressure when all four of them get going." She chewed on her bottom lip. "They've been bugging me for years to settle down."

I took a deep breath, "Don't you think this could work as a solution to get them off your back as well? Even if it's only temporary, it takes that stress off your shoulders for a little while." I felt like I was grasping at straws. The more holes she poked in my plan, the less confident I felt about it.

"So, you want to fake date me to convince my mother and my best friends that we are together? Do you know what that entails?"

I shrugged, "I assume it involves showing up, smiling when appropriate, and not trying to stick my hand under your dress."

She grimaced at the subtle mention of her disaster date from last night. It was a low blow, but I needed something to drive the point home. "If only it were that simple. My mother and my friends won't be convinced by one night. There are pre-wedding brunches, rehearsal dinners, and Christmas parties. This wedding is basically a month-long Christmas festival, and my mother is coordinating all of it. Starting tomorrow."

"I'm aware."

"You'd have to attend everything."

"I expected that."

"And deal with my mother."

"I'm sure I've dealt with worse." My mind flickered back to my own parents, my never impressed, always stoic father, and my loving but mentally absent mother, and it took every ounce of my self-control not to shudder.

"Why?" she demanded, uncrossing her legs and leaning forward. "Why me?"

Something about you intrigues me. Because you looked lonely in a way that I recognize. Because you deserve someone in your corner, even if it's temporary. Because the pain I saw in your eyes last night haunts me. Because something in me won't let go.

That's what I wanted to say, but from the look of distrust on her face, I knew she wouldn't believe any of that. Hell, I hardly believed it myself.

I didn't say any of that. Instead, I leaned back in my chair, trying hard to school my features into something neutral and emotionless. Something that wouldn't betray how awkward this moment felt for me. I was used to business deals. I could handle a merger or negotiation or high stakes moment in my sleep, but this felt different. It felt like there was more to lose, even though I couldn't figure out what that was.

"Because it benefits us both. The investors want to see stability, and you need a date to get your people off your back. It's mutually convenient."

"Convenient," she repeated, skeptical.

"And," I add, "I'm good at pretending."

Something flickered in her expression as she studied me, really studied me, as if she was trying to read between the lines. I sat still, holding her gaze in a steady and unwavering one of my own. Even though my heart was thumping loudly in my chest.

"If we do this, we have to make it believable."

"We will." I responded, with a confidence I didn't quite feel.

"We have to do it all the way."

I didn't know what that meant, but I nodded anyway, "Agreed."

"If this is a clever way to get in my bed, you can save it." She narrowed her eyes at me.

"I wouldn't dream of it." I replied, which...wasn't completely true.

"Fine, Clairfield. We've got a deal. Just don't piss me off."

I offered her my hand and for a moment, she stared at it, without moving. As if she wanted to take back everything we had agreed on and kick me out of her office. Honestly, I wouldn't blame her if she did. Just as my confidence began to drain and I considered pulling my hand back and leaving, she sighed, placing her hand gingerly in mine and giving it a firm shake.

"Glad we understand each other." I grinned.

"Hmph," she replied. But something in her smile told me that we don't understand a thing. And something in my chest whispered that "pretend" may not stay pretend for long.

3

Deja

Dear Diary,

When a woman carries her heart like a fragile ornament, she learns to wrap it in glitter and good sense. She shines it up, holds it high, and hopes the world will see the sparkle instead of the cracks.

But the one meant for her does not fall for the shine. He will notice the places she's patched with humor, the softness beneath her sharp edges. He will see her when she is unguarded, undone, or unexpectedly honest and he will not turn away.

He will meet her in a moment that feels too real, too raw, too close and something in her will recognize him even before her pride does. Pay attention. Love often enters through the side door, wearing an unfamiliar face.

After the unexpected meeting with Rashaad and this diary entry that popped up when I got home from work, my brain was running a mile a minute. A fake dating situation was not on my bingo card, but it would solve my problems for the moment. It'd give me a chance to get through this wedding and into the new year without the same probing comments from my mother about why I never found anyone suitable.

I never thought I'd be the type to have a fake dating trope, and the idea of fooling my friends and my family did give me a rush of excitement. I was tired of the pitying looks from my girls. They meant well, but after this journal had matched them all up, even Monae, the most painfully logical and literal one of the five of us, was starry-eyed over her man.

The only one left dateless was me. Usually, that wouldn't bother me. I had no problem rotating through the roster and finding new people to occupy my time, but seeing my girls all booed up for the holidays was starting to bum me out. I had resigned myself to the fact that I would have no one and would have to power through these Christmas and wedding moments by myself. At least, until Rashaad stepped in and offered to be my knight in shining armor.

I wasn't sure if I fully believed his excuse about it being a mutually beneficial decision, but who was I to look a gift horse in the mouth? He could schmooze with his investors, and I could avoid having my mother try to hook me up with every man that wasn't immediately attached to someone. I know she was just trying to help in the only way she knew how, but it was doing the exact opposite. It was giving desperate. I may be a lot of things, but desperate will never be one of them.

I sighed and looked at my reflection in the bathroom mirror.

Adobe sat at my feet, staring up at me with the dopey-eyed wonder that could only come from a boy dog. I smiled down at him, getting a little serotonin boost from him staring at me like I was the best thing he'd ever seen in his life, even though I was currently looking like I had been ridden hard and hung up wet. My silver bonnet was twisted sideways on my head, real life proof of the fitful night of sleep I had. But there was no time to obsess over what that entry could mean or why Rashaad popped up suddenly willing to help me solve my problems; today was the first day of December, which meant the wedding festivities would be in full swing. We all had to meet Elodie at the bridal shop in a few hours for the final dress fittings and unfortunately, my mother would be in attendance as well.

I didn't understand why the wedding coordinator needed to be invited to the dress fitting in the first place, but that was Elodie's choice and she was too kindhearted to tell my mother no. I could only imagine how she strong-armed her way into the fitting, giving some type of excuse about needing to see the dresses so she could plan for the smaller details.

I pulled off my bonnet and grabbed my toothbrush. I could get through the dress fitting, and then Rashaad and I would be meeting for lunch to strategize. All I had to do was make it through this. It didn't take me long to finish getting ready and head out to the bridal shop. Luckily, it was only a few minutes away from my house.

Elodie and I had just pulled back from the hug and reached for Audrey when Monae and Brina came rushing in like someone was chasing them. I always loved having my girls with me. No matter what we were doing, their presence made everything better.

If there's anything more humbling than fluorescent lighting, it's fluorescent lighting in a bridal boutique while wearing a dress that could double as a disco ball. The sparkles on these dresses were beautiful, but blinding. I caught every bit of lighting with even the slightest of movements.

"Okay, ladies!" Amada, Elodie's grandmother, called, clapping her hands. "Let's see those gowns."

We stepped out, one by one, and suddenly the room looked like Christmas ornaments on display. The gold of our dresses and the red of Audrey's caught the light like we were auditioning to be Mariah Carey's background singers on a Christmas special. I felt like a trophy, but a stunning one, nonetheless.

"Twirl, baby," my mother demanded, as if she was the director of the moment. "I need to see the fit from all angles."

I gave a half-hearted spin. "You're the wedding coordinator, Ma. Not the costume designer."

"I am the mother of a bridesmaid," she said pointedly. "Which means everything my child wears is a direct reflection of me."

I sighed, not wanting to fight with her in the middle of Elodie's moment. This wasn't about me at all. This was about my girl getting to marry the love of her life after the sweetest romance I'd ever seen in person.

Ms. Amada placed a gentle hand on my arm and smiled at me when I glanced up at her. As if she could sense my internal struggle. "Gold looks beautiful on you, dear. It catches your undertones perfectly."

I smiled back, appreciative of the encouragement. "Okay, El!

Don't keep us waiting forever, girl!" I called out.

Elodie stepped into the room, and for a moment, she didn't even look real. She looked like a painting that had come to life. Every detail of the dress was crafted to make her look like she'd been born for this exact moment. The bodice hugged her, the lace curling over her skin in delicate patterns that seemed to breathe as she moved.

The off-the-shoulder sleeves were sheer, intricate, and wrapped down her arms with each embroidered flower catching the light. The skirt flowed around her in a sweeping cascade of tulle and lace with floral appliques drifting downward from her waist and dissolving into the airy layers of the gown. When she took a step, the train followed behind her like a quiet sigh. She looked magical and absolutely breathtaking.

Silence fell over us as we stared at our best friend, emotions heavy and intense throughout the room. I was overcome with happiness for my girl. She didn't just look like a bride; she looked like a woman fully stepping into her own magic.

"Is it too much?" she asked, after the silence had stretched too long.

"You look..." I began and then stopped, too choked up to speak.

"Breathtaking," Brina finished for me.

"Mekhi is a lucky man." Ms. Amada smiled, stepping closer to her granddaughter. "I wish your grandfather was here to see this."

Tears welled in Elodie's eyes. "Me too," she whispered.

The four of us surrounded Elodie, trying not to get our sequins snagged on the delicate lace of her dress. "I can't believe this is really happening." Audrey sighed.

"I'm actually getting married in two weeks." Elodie's eyes widened, as if it was finally hitting her and then she beamed, practically vibrating with joy. All eyes were focused on her, which was exactly the distraction I needed.

"Oh, I'm bringing a date after all," I said casually, maybe too casually.

The room froze as if someone pressed the pause button. My heart thumped loudly in my chest.

Monae raised an eyebrow, "A date? You?"

"Wow," I said looking at all of them, "the confidence y'all have in my romantic prospects is overwhelming."

Elodie clapped her hands, squealing. "A holiday romance! I knew it! The journal is working!"

"Um yeah. Something like that. I'm actually meeting him for lunch after we finish up here."

My mother cut in, laser focused. I'd almost forgotten she was here. "Finally. Someone to keep you occupied and maybe convince you to dress age-appropriately for once."

"Ma." I sighed, exasperated.

"What? I'm simply saying a good man will encourage you to tone things down."

The girls all crowded closer, ignoring my mother. Amada glared at her, but said nothing.

"So," Audrey began, "You have a date, but you're being weird about it."

"I'm not being weird."

"You definitely are." Elodie tilted her head, staring at me with that stern teacher glare she had mastered over the years, "Is this the guy from the other night? The one that got too handsy?"

"No, definitely not. This is someone else. It's...Rashaad, actually."

"Clairfield?" Brina piped up. "Langston's business partner?"

"Yeah. We met the other night while I was on a date with the handsy guy. He was there for a business meeting. We kind of hit it off." It wasn't completely a lie. We did meet that night. He witnessed my humiliation in person but was kind enough not to press when I didn't want to talk about it.

"What does the journal say about it?" Monae asked.

I rolled my eyes. "It's being cryptic, honestly. I have no idea what to make of the entries so far. Kinda out here shooting in the dark."

"Langston is always talking about how excited he is for Rashaad to meet someone who will knock him off his game." Brina grinned. "Who better than you, Deja?"

Before I could respond the tailor stepped out from the back and ushered the girls back onto the platforms to begin hem measurements. I took a step forward, ready to be up on the platform, when my mother's hand clamped around my elbow.

"Come with me for a second," she murmured, pulling me behind her. Her smile reserved for the public, pleasant on the surface and sharp underneath, was plastered on her face like a mask. I sighed and followed her behind the curtain, trying to brace myself for what I knew was about to shatter what was left of my mood.

We stepped behind a curtain and into a small side room with spare veils and extra bridesmaid dresses. The second we were by ourselves; she sighed like the weight of the world was resting on her thin shoulders.

"A date, Deja Mielle?"

"Yes, Mother. A Date. Why is that so unheard of?"

She sighed, folding her arms. "It's not unheard of. I just wish you would have told me."

"Why would I need your permission?" I tried hard to keep my tone respectful, but I could feel my irritation growing. "It doesn't even concern you. Not really."

"It becomes my concern when people start asking questions," she shot back, "I'm coordinating this wedding for your friend as a favor to you. I need to know what to expect."

I blinked at her, confused. "Who exactly is going to give a second thought to my dating life at Elodie's wedding?"

"All the mothers." She sniffed. "All the aunties. All the extended relatives. They're all going to want to know about the loudest bridesmaid covered in tattoos. You stand out whether you like it or not and it gets to be exhausting defending your...choices."

Her words stung. It was a familiar bruise, a reoccurring argument that still managed to suck all of the air out of the room.

I crossed my own arms, matching her stance. "What choices, Ma?"

She said nothing, but her eyes gave everything away. As she

flicked her gaze down my body, eyeing my curves, my tattoos, my sparkle, the unspoken judgment stood between us like a third person. It was always there, always lingering, waiting for a moment to pounce when it could cause the most damage to my confidence.

"I'm not going to apologize for having a personality," I snapped, trying to keep my voice low. "Just because I'm not exactly who you had in mind for a daughter, doesn't mean that I am somehow defective."

"I'm not saying you're defective and I'm not asking you to apologize." She rolled her eyes as if I was a small child throwing a tantrum. "I'm asking you to be realistic."

"What does *that* mean?"

She stepped closer and placed her hands on my shoulders. "You're a beautiful girl, my Deja. Talented. Smart. But you don't have to be so...loud. Leave room for a man to lead."

I swallowed the lump in my throat. I knew she meant well. I knew she thought she was protecting me, but every word smacked against my self-esteem and sank like a stone. Dragging me down with it.

"You think it's my fault I'm alone," I whispered, the realization curling around me, sucking the air out of my lungs.

Her lips pressed together. "I think you hide the best parts of yourself behind theatrics. And yes, I worry that makes it harder for someone to take you seriously."

On the other side of the curtain, my friends were laughing. Easy, light, carefree while I was standing there glittering from head to toe, feeling like a cracked Christmas ornament my mother was desperately trying to glue back together, even though she was the one that broke it in the first place. It had taken the last bit of my energy to power through this conversation without crumpling, and now, I just wanted to cancel the lunch with Rashaad, go back home and hide away from the world. I wanted to hide away from the people that demanded too much of me, because right now, I didn't feel like I had anything left to give.

Her expression softened, "I just want the best for you. I love you."

A single tear slipped down my cheek. "I know. I just wish your version of best wasn't so small."

By the time I pulled up to the little bistro Rashaad had texted me the address to, I'd convinced myself that I was fine. Though my mother's words cut through every piece of armor I'd put around my heart, I could let it roll off my shoulders and keep moving. I parked my car and then stepped out, surveying the spot from the outside. It looked like one of those airy places with too much natural light and overpriced salads.

I spotted him immediately when I stepped inside. He was leaning back in that maddeningly relaxed way men only pull off when they're born without the "try too hard" gene. His locs were pulled up in a messy bun on the top of his head, exposing that sharp jawline. The olive-green shirt he wore made his skin glow in the ugly light of the restaurant. It almost made me feel underdressed. I glanced down at my wine-colored sweater dress, debating whether I should run home, change and then come back. He turned when I came in, as if he sensed my presence, and stood.

"Hey." I smiled.

"Hey." His eyes stayed on me a beat too long. Observing. Reading. Annoyingly perceptive. "You good?"

"You ask me that a lot," I quipped, sliding into the chair he pulled out for me.

"And yet, you never give me a genuine answer."

I ignored his comment and grabbed the menu. I didn't come here to be scrutinized. I get enough of that from my mother. I came because we needed to discuss the game plan for this fake dating scheme.

"Hi. I'm Jenna, your waitress, what can I get you to drink?" The young blonde girl seemed to materialize out of thin air.

"Water, please." I smiled. "And I'll have the Bistro Burger and the fries. Burger should be medium-well, extra pickles on the side please. As many pickles as you can spare."

"I'll have the same. Minus the pickles." Rashaad said when she turned to him. She nodded, grabbed our menus and then bounced off to the kitchen to put in the orders. I was hoping the interruption would offer a natural shift in conversation, but it didn't.

"Out with it."

"Why do you care so much?" I shot back.

"We gotta sell this, right? Pretend like we are really together," he replied smoothly, seemingly unfazed by my aggressive tone.

"So, we need to get to know each other."

I didn't come here intending to talk about my mother cornering me and cutting open every insecurity I worked overtime to hide. I came here to be the version of myself I knew how to control; the sharp, unbothered, glossy version. But the way he was looking at me was like he somehow saw past all of that.

"What happened?" he asked quietly.

Something in his tone unhooked me, just a little, and I let my shoulders sag in defeat. It'd taken so much energy to get through the rest of the fitting with a smile, without tipping my girls off that something was wrong, that I didn't have anything left to pretend anymore. It was too much.

I exhaled. "We had the final fitting this morning. And my mother was there."

He nodded like he already expected that. "And?"

I looked away, staring at the people eating on the other side of the restaurant. "And she reminded me, again, that people expect things from me. And if I slip, even a little, it reflects on her. She's tired of defending my choices."

"What choices?"

I wave a hand down my body. "The way I dress. The tattoos. The loud, glittery personality. The assertiveness. It's such a burden that I'm so different and she's concerned that I'm making everything so much harder on myself." I rolled my eyes, even though repeating the words hurt, "I'm alone because it's my fault."

He said nothing, just listened as I detailed the most hurtful parts of the conversation. When I was done venting, the feeling of something wet hitting my hand surprised me. I glanced down to realize that the wetness was tears. I hadn't realized I'd begun to cry. Rashaad handed me a napkin and waited for me to wipe my eyes. I sniffled, embarrassed that this was now the third time he'd seen me without my usual persona. He was threatening my reputation without even realizing it.

"That sounds heavy," he said finally. "Unfair."

I blinked at him. "You're not gonna say she meant well?"

"No." He shook his head slowly. "Because even if she did… that's still a hell of a weight and expectation to dump on you."

A shocked, tiny laugh escapes me. "Wow. You really aren't normal."

"Most men aren't allowed to be," he answered, only half joking.

Then he leaned back, fingers laced together on the table, his eyes never leaving mine.

"I get it, you know. The pressure." His voice dropped. "My parents, especially my dad, they expect perfection. Always. The oldest son, the responsible one, the one who never messes up, never complains, never has emotions." He scoffs softly. "Being 'strong' becomes a job, not a trait. And sometimes that job becomes exhausting."

I stared at him, the confession hitting harder than I expected and connecting with something deep inside.

"I didn't know that," I said quietly.

"Why would you?" His mouth lifted in a small, warm smile. "I don't go around announcing my internal struggles during business meetings. Makes things too awkward."

That pulled a genuine laugh out of me, temporarily lifting the mood. I looked down at the table, even though I wasn't really seeing it.

"You don't have to be perfect with me," he continued. "There is no expectation of perfection. Be whoever you need to be."

"Right now, I need to be two bites deep into this burger. I am starving." I deflected, desperately wanting to change the subject. I didn't expect to be seen so fully on a fake first date. He seemed to sense that I no longer wanted to talk about it and nodded.

"Their burgers are pretty solid. I think you'll like them."

"So now that we've laid my burdens bare, tell me about your day." I said. I took a sip of the water the waitress had placed on the table at some point during the conversation and tried my best to look like I hadn't just been crying.

"It was chill. We recently secured Draymond Bell with Bell Investments. So Langston has been living off that high for the last few days." Rashaad rolled his eyes, even though there was a hint of amusement in his tone and expression.

"Getting to the bag. Not mad at that."

He laughed. "That's what I'm good at, securing the money while he makes the designs."

"Have you ever considered doing something else?"

"No. There's no need. Langston is my boy on top of being a business partner. We work well together. It's a well-oiled machine. Well...it is now anyway."

"You mean after that whole Kalyse thing?" I asked. "Brina told me about it. That was a tough case for everyone."

He nodded. "She shook his confidence for a bit, but he's slowly getting back to how he moved before."

The waitress sat two piping hot burgers down in front of us with a smile. My mouth watered, looking at my plate. In my anxiousness to get to the dress fitting, I'd skipped breakfast and now I was paying for it. My stomach growled as if pissed at me for not feeding it sooner.

"Oh, this burger is fire," I groaned as soon as I took a bite.

He laughed. "I told you."

Eating lunch with Rashaad was refreshing in a way I hadn't expected. It was enough to make me almost forget everything my mother had said at the dress fitting. By the time lunch was over, we had talked about everything under the sun. From our jobs to our hobbies, to our fears and regrets.

Talking to him came naturally and gave me a chance to really let down my guard. It felt like we had known each other for years, instead of just short of a month.

"Guilty pleasure show," Rashaad asked, dipping a spoonful into his ice cream. We'd stepped out for a quick dessert at the ice cream shop down the street from the bistro.

"Bob's Burgers," I replied easily. "I am pretty sure I've watched it all the way through at least four different times. What about yours?"

"Everybody Hates Chris. Black women and the way they gravitate to Bob's Burgers should be studied." He reached out and stuck his spoon in my ice cream, scooping out a big helping and shoving it in his mouth with a slick grin.

"Hey!" I shouted, sliding it out of his reach. "You have plenty of your own."

"Yours tastes better. Favorite Christmas tradition?"

"I always buy one really ugly ornament."

"Why?"

"My grandfather started it as a joke. He gave everybody in the family one ornament, and it was always ugly. One time he gave me a stick of butter ornament." I smiled at the memory. "I kept up the tradition when he passed. The ugliest ornament I can find. Every time."

"My family has a gingerbread house decorating competition. It gets pretty intense. Takes weeks of planning sometimes. We have judges and they take votes. It's a whole thing."

"What does the winner get?" I asked.

"Bragging rights for the year and a visa gift card."

"That sounds like a lot of fun."

When we finished our ice cream, Rashaad walked with me back to my car. If I was honest with myself, I'd admit that I wasn't ready for this to end. I enjoyed his company. Not to mention he was a gorgeous man. Even now in his plain green t-shirt and dark jeans, he looked ready to step on a runway if the situation called for it. It was hard to believe that someone like him wasn't already locked down in a committed relationship.

"So, why are you single?" I blurted as we approached my car.

"I could ask you the same question."

"You first."

"It takes a special kind of woman to make me want to leave singlehood behind. I'm not sure she exists yet and if she does, I want to make sure that I'm ready for her."

For some reason, his words stung just a little. It took a special man to make me want to leave singlehood behind as well, but hearing the words come from him made me sad.

"I hope you meet her one day."

He glanced down at me, saying nothing, but somehow seeing deep into my soul. I wasn't sure if venting to him about my complicated relationship with my mother made me feel oddly close to him, but it was more than I was ready to sort through at this exact moment.

"I hope so too," he replied, leaning forward, and I found myself stepping closer, shrinking the distance between us. I closed my eyes, bracing myself for a kiss I hadn't realized until this moment that I really wanted, but it never came. The click of my car door opening brought me back to reality and I opened my eyes, embarrassed.

He was watching me, a look of amusement coloring his features. I wanted to evaporate where I stood. I had completely misread that moment and ended up embarrassed, for the second time today.

"So, I'll see you tomorrow for the Christmas brunch? Make sure you wear your ugliest Christmas sweater." I smiled, hoping to distract from the moment.

"I'll be there. Text me your address so I can pick you up."

The thought of him knowing where I lived made me giddy and slightly nervous. I wanted to squeal like an excited high school girl, but instead I slipped into my car and turned on the engine. Rashaad shut the door behind me and stepped back. With a small wave, I pulled out of the parking lot and headed home, trying to push the sudden and intense desire to see what his lips tasted like, out of my mind.

"Hello, my blushing bride!" I sang happily into the phone. Elodie's name had popped up across my screen while I was relaxing with Adobe on my couch.

"Hey, girl. You got a second?" The seriousness in her voice made me pause.

"For you? I've got two seconds. What's wrong? You good?"

She sighed. "I am, but I wanted to make sure you were okay. My grandma told me about the conversation with your mom earlier. I guess she'd overheard some of it."

"Oh."

"I was wondering why you seemed so...off...afterwards. Are you okay?"

I waved a hand, trying to push away the question, even though she couldn't see me. "Of course I am, babe. Why wouldn't I be?"

"Dej, I'm serious."

"My mom and I have a strained relationship, but it's nothing for you to worry about." I chewed on my lip. "I'm serious. I'm fine."

"Why didn't you tell me? I never would have hired her to

coordinate, if you'd have-"

"That's exactly why I didn't tell you. As crazy as she makes me, Denise Johnson is the best in the game when it comes to this. I want my girl to have the very best."

Elodie's voice grew quiet. "I want you to be okay, too, though."

"I am." Adobe nuzzled his warm nose into my leg, as his way of telling me I'd been on the phone too long and he wanted more attention. I rubbed his head absentmindedly. "I promise, El, I'm good. I just want you to have the best wedding possible. Don't worry about me."

"Only if you're sure." She still sounded skeptical. "I can easily tell her that I no longer need her."

"I would never hear the end of that. Don't do that. I appreciate you though."

"Of course. Has the journal said anything else?"

As if it heard itself be mentioned, the soft rustling sound began from where the journal sat on my counter. I turned in time to catch the pages flipping.

I laughed, getting off the couch and walking over to it. "I think you just woke it up."

"What does it say?" The excitement in her voice was undeniable. I waited while the pages finished flipping, my own excitement bubbling inside me. Would this be the journal entry that points me in the direction of my true love? Someone who won't ask me to be anything other than myself? For the rest of my girls, the journal was painfully obvious, full of puns and blaring signs pointing in the direction of the person they were meant to be with. For me, so far, the entries felt more subtle. As if it was a riddle I was meant to solve on my own.

I took a deep breath and read the words out loud:

Dear Diary,

The words from her mother struck deeper than she lets anyone see. But today, someone noticed anyway.

He saw past the sparkles and the snark that she hides behind and recognized the weight she carried, not because she slipped, but because he was always meant to see it. That only happens when two souls carrying similar burdens find a frequency that fits.

Do not fear this shift. When the time comes, the one destined for her heart will see her in her most unguarded light and choose her still. If she allows herself to be seen.

4

Rashaad

"Did you secure a date to this wedding?" Langston demanded, as soon as I picked up the phone. Didn't even bother with a hello. "I need you there, Rashaad."

"And hello to you too." I replied, closing the front door behind me. I'd just made it home from spending time with Deja and here he comes, swooping in to dampen the mood. I shouldn't have answered the phone when I saw his name on the screen. A glutton for punishment, I guess.

"I'm serious, man. I got a look at the guest list, and a lot of potentials have RSVPd. I need you presentable, polite, and not glaring at anybody."

"Glaring?" I repeated dryly, "I do not glare."

"Have you seen your face lately?" Langston laughed. "Ninety-eight percent of the time, you're glaring. You're sleeping for the other two percent and there's no guarantee you aren't mean mugging the pillow in your dreams."

"Cap. Anyway, yes, I did get a date. So you can stop panicking. I'm a man of my word, you know this."

"True. Anyone I know?"

I paused, debating whether I wanted to be truthful with him or not. "Yes." I sighed. "It's Deja."

"Bridesmaid Deja?"

"No, nigga, the other one." I rolled my eyes.

"My fault. I'm just surprised. She's a firecracker. Not your usual docile and opinionless type."

I was well aware of how different she was than the usual women I picked, but that was only because I'd been looking for a good time not a long time. It was much easier to get in and get out when there was nothing of substance between the ears. Deja was different. Hell, she was different than anyone I'd ever met. Non-romantic connections included.

"You didn't say I needed to make a love connection. Just get a date. She'll be busy with wedding bull, and I can use that opportunity to work the room."

"Hm." He hummed, sounding as if he didn't really believe my reasoning. "I don't know man, you might mess around and end up falling for this girl. She different, different."

If only he knew how correct he was.

"I can handle myself, Langston." I shot back, a little sharper than I had intended.

He picked up on the change in my tone and paused. "Don't get caught slipping, is all I'm saying."

"I hear you."

"So, I guess that means I'll see you at this ornament decorating thing in the next few days,." he said, after the silence stretched on a beat too long.

"You will."

"Good. It should be lowkey, just the wedding party and you. Can't wait to see you and Dej-"

"I'm hanging up now," I interrupted, pulling the phone away from my ear. I could hear him laughing as I clicked the end call button and ended the conversation. I had too much on my mind and I didn't need him trying to psychoanalyze me.

I told myself I wouldn't think about her after our lunch. I told myself I'd get in my car, drive back to my house, and pretend like the entire conversation didn't stick to me like warm syrup. And yet, here I was, hours later, sitting on my couch replaying the look on her face when she leaned in for a kiss that I didn't reciprocate.

Did I want to? Yes. Of course. I am a man with two working eyes. She's gorgeous in a way you don't come across often. Not in real life. But I didn't want to complicate things. I had a job to do and a goal to meet, adding feelings to something that was strictly business would do nothing but bring headache for the both of us. That was the last thing she needed from me, with everything already on her plate.

But that didn't mean I hadn't considered breaking my self-imposed rule and kissing her. Even throughout lunch and the dessert that followed, I found my gaze drifting back down to her mouth more often than it should have. I felt no better than that cornball I'd seen her on the date with a few days ago, but I couldn't help myself. To deny her beauty was to deny myself air. Absolutely impossible.

Seeing her in this light: relaxed, comfortable, not putting on a facade for anyone, gave me a quick glimpse of the real Deja Johnson and I'd be a fool if I didn't admit I wanted to see more.

For the millionth time, my mind drifted back to the way her entire body responded when I told her that I understood. Like I had physically lifted the burden from her shoulders and placed it on mine, even if it was just temporary. The pressure was something I knew all too well and hearing someone else struggle with the same thing hit me harder than I expected.

Most people talk about pressure like it's a badge of honor. Oldest sibling privilege. Born leader. You're so put together, Rashaad. Meanwhile, my childhood was a series of gentle reminders that I wasn't allowed to break.

"You're the oldest. Handle it."

"Your sister looks up to you. Don't make mistakes."

"Boys don't show emotion, Rashaad. Be strong."

"You can't be soft in a world that was built to break you."

That last one stuck like a commandment. I spent years sharpening myself into something reliable. Something efficient. Something unshakeable. Exactly what Deja tried to be for her friends. Exactly what her mother demanded of her. I ran a hand down my face and leaned back in my chair. This was supposed to be simple. Show up to some holiday events, charm her mother into leaving her alone, help Langston nail new investors, and go home. Light work. But now all I can think about is the way her eyes softened when she realized she could be free with me. I saw past her glitter and snark and right into the version of her she tries to tuck away.

And I liked what I saw. Which was the problem.

I crossed over to my closet and opened it, with no idea what I was searching for. The first wedding related event was coming up in two days, an ornament decorating night with the wedding party. Low-stakes, cozy and festive. Nothing I needed to prepare for. So, naturally, I pulled up her social media. Instagram on my phone screen and her Facebook on my computer at the desk in my bedroom.

That led me down a rabbit hole of information and after two hours of obsessive searching, I'd combed through each one of her friend's pages and their boyfriend's pages. I wanted to make it look like Deja and I were actually serious about being together, and not just playing around until the wedding was over. If I was going to fool her four best friends, especially Brina who was quick to interrogate someone like she was back in the courtroom, I needed to be on my game.

I exited Deja's socials and pulled her number up on my phone to send her a text but then froze with my finger hovering over the button. For once in my life, I wasn't really sure what to say to her. I wanted to be casual but not too casual. She didn't need to know

I was researching her people.

What color are you wearing to the ornament decorating thing?

A few seconds later, my screen lit up with a response from her. I blinked away the little rush of excitement and opened the message.

Burgundy dress, gold shoes. Why?

I glanced up at my closet, landing on a gold sweater that would complement her colors without looking like I was trying too hard.

Making sure I had something to match your fly. Gotta look the part.

Another bubble appeared. Then it stopped. And started again. I watched as she typed, suddenly feeling a pang of nervousness in my chest.

You're taking this fake boyfriend thing seriously.

My lips tilted before I could stop them. I couldn't deny that things felt easy between us. In a carefree, non-judgmental way you could relax into.

I take all my jobs seriously.

I put my phone in my back pocket and walked to my kitchen for a bottle of water I don't actually want. I just need something to do with my hands while my brain ran in circles. I leaned my hip against the counter and surveyed the living room. A half-decorated tree I hadn't had the time to finish, open boxes of ornaments and tangled lights scattered around the floor, waiting for me to pick back up where I'd left off.

I stared at the mess, letting my mind wander back to when I was thirteen. I'd been in my room upset that I didn't get a spot on the football team after I had been running drills and practicing every moment of free time I could find. I'd spent months working on my footwork and making sure I was fast and strong, but it wasn't enough. I'd almost made the cut but not quite; they'd chosen one of the boys who'd gone to the summer camp instead. I remember the coach had told me that it wasn't because I was a bad player, it was just because they already knew how the other guy trained. He promised I had a shot, if I just kept working at it. I knew he was trying to be encouraging and keep me from giving up, but it had been a lot for my thirteen-year-old brain to process.

The denial landed in my chest like a crushing blow, but I waited until I got home in my room to cry. I knew that my father would make it ten times worse if I broke in front of him. Even though I wanted nothing more than to be hugged and given some words of encouragement, that's not what would happen. When I got in the car after the tryouts, my father had folded the newspaper he was reading and laid it across his lap. He studied me in the rearview mirror while I did my best to control the raging emotions inside of me. I was trying and failing to hold it together.

"I know those aren't tears I see on your face, Rashaad." He

turned to look at me in the backseat, slumped forward with my arms crossed around me. "You need to tighten up."

"No sir." I sniffed, even though I was fighting for my life to hold back to the tears.

"Strength isn't optional for you. If you go around crying because things don't go your way, this world will eat you alive, boy!"

My phone buzzed, pulling me out of that moment. It was another text from Deja.

So, should I stick with the dress idea? Or are we thinking pants?

I snorted.

Wear whatever. As long as you don't outshine the tree.

There was a short pause then her response popped up on my screen, making me laugh out loud. This girl was something else. Something special.

I outshine whatever room I walk into. Bold of you to assume I'd do anything less.

I headed back into my bedroom, with a smile on my face, and started gathering things I might need for the ornament event.

I was doing too much and I knew it, but I couldn't stop. This wasn't a tactical mission and didn't require this much attention to detail, but something in me wanted to go in prepared. I wanted to make this easy for Deja so she could relax. I wanted her to feel like she could lean on me without having to explain herself. I wanted her not to regret having chosen me to be her fake date.

The realization made me pause mid-reach, in front of my closet. The sweater was dangling over my shoulder and the pants sat right in front of me. Since when did I care about making things easy for Deja? That wasn't the original mission, but at some point during the lunch, it had replaced the primary mission. This felt more important than kissing up to an investor.

"This is ridiculous," I muttered to myself, "it's not even a real date."

But I still grabbed the pair of pants that matched with the sweater and ironed them. I hung them up in the closet separate from everything else so I could grab it easily, while mentally rehearsing a few small facts about each of the bridesmaids and their dates. I even glanced back through Deja's profile, trying to find things we could relate on and maybe talk about if we had a moment to ourselves.

I researched, I rehearsed, and I made small notes for reference later on. And as silly as this entire thing made me feel, I still prepared for this like it was the most important thing in my life at the moment, because in some ways, it felt like it was.

Two days later, with a venti peppermint mocha in my hand, I stepped up to Deja's front porch and rang the doorbell. If I was honest with myself, I'd admit that I was nervous and a little excited to see Deja again, even though we had seen each other not that long ago and had been texting almost nonstop since. The more we talked and hung out, the more of her time I wanted.

A dog barked wildly on the other side of the door before I heard the patter of soft footsteps. I squared my shoulders just as the door opened and Deja stood in front of me in her dress, and bare feet.

"Hi! I'm running behind. I just need to finish my makeup and I'll be done," she called over her shoulder as she turned and ran back in the direction of what I assumed was her bedroom. The puppy that I'd heard barking bounded happily over to me, tail wagging a mile a minute.

"I brought you coffee," I called out.

Deja came running back out to grab the cup I'd placed on the counter. "You are a godsend." She took a sip and then her eyes widened. "Wait, what is this?"

"A peppermint mocha."

"How did you know I loved these?"

"I did my research." I smiled. Luckily for me, she was very open on social media. Not on a creepy level, but just enough for guys like me who paid attention to even the smallest details could pick up on some things.

"Wow," was all she said. I couldn't quite read the look on her face. Did I do too much too soon?

The puppy, sick of being ignored, let out a yip and nudged my free hand with his nose. I glanced down to see him staring up at me, tail still wagging faster than the speed of light.

"What's up, little guy?" I asked, reaching down to scratch him behind the ears. He danced happily, too excited to sit still long enough for me to really pet him.

"That's Adobe. We're learning to be polite and not jump on people."

"Hi, Adobe."

I watched, amused while the puppy danced around my legs and then hopped up like he could climb me if I let him. I had been meaning to get a dog of my own, but I hadn't had the time to get to the shelter. Maybe I could just help Deja with him and that would count as my dog. I made a mental note to ask what kind of treats he liked so I could pick some up on the way home. Maybe I could grab a toy or two and replenish the dog food supply that I saw in the corner, it was looking a little low and-

I froze. Did I really just adopt Deja's dog in my head? The fact that I slipped into that mindset so quickly threw me for a loop and made me want to step back outside and run to my car. It felt like too much too quickly. Instead, I shook the thought away and forced myself to look around Deja's spot.

The walls were drenched in a deep velvety burgundy that seemed to drink in the light. It made the space feel both intimate and commanding. A chandelier hung above my head with crystal droplets shimmering with warm light, each one casting soft reflections against the dark ceiling.

The couch was massive, black, and plush. It somehow anchored

the space with quiet power. Pillows in different shades of berry and red decorated the couch. The entire living room felt like it was meant for big moments. For people to share secrets over dark liquor and dim lighting. It felt like brazen opulence in the best way possible.

"This is a dope spot," I called out, looking around. "I've never seen an all-black Christmas tree."

Deja hooked her earrings in and smiled up at me. "Not too much?"

"Definitely not." I answered quickly, maybe too quickly. "It's very you. Bold. Daring. Elegant."

She stared at me for a minute; something flickered across her expression that I wanted to reach for but decided against. I'd meant what I said. I didn't want her to change a thing.

She cleared her throat. "We should probably get going. Elodie will have my ass if I'm late again."

I nodded and followed her outside to my car.

I don't know who decided ornament decorating counted as light and relaxing, but clearly they've never watched five black women wield glitter glue and bows like weapons. The minute we arrived, Deja was swallowed by Brina, Audrey, and Monae. They were all talking at the same time and throwing curious glances over their shoulders at me while I stood in the doorway with my hands in my pockets awkwardly.

"Everyone, this is Rashaad. My-" Her voice faltered for a split second. "My date."

I acknowledged the room and greeted each person as they

introduced themselves. Then stood behind Deja like an awkward bodyguard while they pelted her with excited questions. Not even caring that I could hear every word. Watching them interact did make me smile. It reminded me a lot of how my sister behaved with her group of friends. Briefly, I considered what it would be like to have Deja meet my little sister. Would they mesh well? Or would it be weird? I had trouble believing that there was someone on this planet that Deja couldn't eventually win over. Her personality had the power to pull people in. It pulled me in almost immediately.

"Ladies, Ladies, please." Deja cut in, smiling brightly, "I'm fragile."

The four of them cackled and wandered over to Elodie who was fully calm and serene, sitting at the counter basking in that "bride-to-be" glow. Mekhi stood close, talking with a young boy who looked to be in his late teens. From the research I'd done, I gathered that this was Kellan, Mekhi and Elodie's foster turned adopted son. A few Christmases ago, Mekhi had taken in Kellan as an emergency foster and apparently, they clicked so well that neither one of them wanted him to leave. It was heartwarming to see how this group of people rallied around this child in need and gave him the family he desperately needed.

I nodded at the two of them and they returned the gesture. At some point, I would introduce myself and get their full story, but right now my focus was getting through this thing without making either of us look bad. Langston and two of the other guys, Jai and Montrell, stood nearby, arranging the paints. He clocked me immediately and gave me a smug smile, making me want to smack it off his face.

I absentmindedly follow Deja over to the decorating table. She reached for a clear ornament, giggling to her friends about wedding details, but the box snagged on the bracelet she was wearing. I heard her mutter something under her breath and then tug lightly at her bracelet. It wouldn't budge and before my brain could connect with my hands, I was untangling it for her.

Everyone noticed. The room got quiet and I tried not to freeze in fear. One of the women, I think it was Audrey, based on my previous research, raised an eyebrow so high I'm surprised it was still connected to her face.

"Okay, attentive!" She giggled, tapping her fingers together in an approving motion.

I pretended I didn't hear her and handed Deja the ornament she was reaching for. Our hands brushed slightly, and I glanced up at her to see her watching me curiously. I couldn't quite read her expression, but I knew she was struggling with something. She eyed me, chewing on her bottom lip before speaking.

Her voice was soft. "Thank you."

There was an array of bows, ribbons, glitter, and sequins to decorate each of the ornaments. I scanned the table and picked out a few things and then sat down next to Deja on the couch. She eyed my selections.

"Burgundy?" she asked.

I glanced down at the ornaments only to notice that I'd picked mostly burgundy as the color choice. I shrugged, like it was the simplest thing in the world. "It's your favorite color."

She blinked, surprised. "I never told you that."

"Your entire living room is a burgundy color scheme, your dress is burgundy, so is your car." I listed off the things one by one. "I just guessed. Wasn't hard."

Her friends stared at me like I just stood on the coffee table and announced her social security number to the room. Langston was watching from where he stood next to Montrell and that smug smile from earlier reappeared. I glanced away, suddenly feeling embarrassed and like I was being ogled like a science experiment.

"Is it giving husband material?" Brina asked, throwing a knowing glance over at Langston who raised his glass in agreement.

"I think so, friend." Monae giggled. Her date, Jai, offered me a sympathetic look. As if he knew exactly what I was in for. Deja coughed, hard enough to choke. She was flustered. I could see her struggle to play it off, but she was unable to find a comeback.

"Please ignore them." She rolled her eyes, after a minute of silent floundering, the bright smile back on her face. "They get a consistent dick for once and then think everything is a fairytale."

Laughter erupted, thankfully pulling the attention away from me and Deja. Conversations about the wedding began, leaving me to relax a little and focus on decorating an ornament. It turns out, the ornaments we decorated would be used on the tree that was a part of Elodie and Mekhi's wedding decorations. Apparently, she is a huge Christmas fan and while he doesn't care as much about the holiday, he was willing to do whatever it took to make her happy.

"What design are you going for?" I asked quietly, nudging my shoulder softly against hers.

She pulled back from her ornament to observe it dramatically,

"Something classy and timeless. Something that says, 'elegant but approachable.' It aligns with my personal branding."

She wiggled her eyebrows, and I laughed before I could stop myself.

"That's a very you way to describe an ornament." I grinned. She flashed a smile back at me and the sight tugged at a part of me I hadn't thought about in ages. "What do you think of mine?"

I held it up so she could get a good look at it. I'd tried to keep the design simple, mostly because my thoughts were occupied elsewhere, but I was proud of it. I didn't usually do this type of thing, creative stuff was more of Langston's ballpark than mine, but I was having a good time here surrounded by Deja and her friends.

"Yours is actually pretty good." She nodded at my ornament, an impressed look on her face.

"Should I be offended at your surprise?"

"Yes." she said, without shame. "I expected you to be trash at this. I thought you'd make something boring. Like corporate blue or something dull and gray."

"I'm not a robot, Deja."

"That's debatable."

I shook my head, laughing. "This fake relationship is going to be the death of me, isn't it?"

She glanced up at me, eyes warm and teasing. "Probably, but don't worry, I'll try to keep the sparkle at a low level."

"Don't," I replied quickly.

She glanced up at me and the look on her face made my heartbeat pick up in a way that had nothing to do with the fumes from the glitter glue. The idea of Deja Johnson dulling her sparkle for anyone, least of all me, was enough to piss me off. There was nothing and no one on this earth worth that.

She stared at me for a moment, chewing on her lip, before she nodded. "Okay."

It was all she said before turning back to her ornament, but in that single word, I heard everything she wasn't saying. I heard the way her voice caught on the last bit of the word, letting me know that I'd flustered her. I forced myself to look away from her and focused on the ornament in front of me, but my mind began to race. My heart was thumping against my ribcage, feeling like I'd just gotten done running a marathon.

I shouldn't want her like this. We had just started this fake dating thing. We were only on date two and I already could feel myself falling, craving more moments where I caught a glimpse of the real her. The version of her that she tucked away and saved for when she was by herself. I was already looking forward to the next time we could be around each other, like a lovesick idiot. I shouldn't be feeling any of this already. But I was.

God, I was.

"I had a great time tonight. I think my friends like you." Deja grinned, leaning against my car door. It was three hours later, and I'd just dropped her off back at her house. Instead of going inside, however, she turned and walked over to my side of the car, leaning into my open window.

"They seem cool. I'm sure your group chat is going to be going off all night."

"My phone has been buzzing nonstop since we pulled out of the driveway." She laughed. "I'm sure they're all going to have a ton of questions I don't have answers for."

"Should we come up with a story?"

She shook her head, waving away my question. "I am quick on my feet. I can handle it."

I grinned, noting how the light from the streetlamp reflected off the side of her face. God, this woman is breathtaking. It wasn't fair. How was I supposed to stay on task when beauty personified stood next to me?

"So, what's next?"

"Dinner at my parents' house tomorrow night." She rolled her eyes. "They won't be as easy as my friends. At least, my mom won't."

"I can handle your mom."

"You say that now." She scoffed. "Just wait."

Even though her tone was light, I could sense a hint of fear in the undertone. She was nervous, maybe even more nervous than she realized. It made me want to shield her from whatever it was that her mother would throw in her direction. It took a lot to rattle Deja, so I could only imagine what I was in for with dinner, but whatever it was, I had her back. Even if it felt weird to admit out loud.

"Do you want to come to the gingerbread house contest?" I blurted, surprising the both of us.

"With your family?" She tilted her head as if she hadn't heard me.

I nodded. "Yeah. My mom makes a deep-fried turkey afterwards that will rock your world. I guarantee it."

"It's got nothing on the honey-glazed ham my dad makes." She leaned in even closer like she had a secret, "It's made people cry before."

"Alright I'll take that bet. So, what do you say? You down?" I held my breath while she considered, not wanting to pressure her but hoping with everything in me that she would say yes.

"You know what? Yes. I'm down."

"Cool." I tried to sound nonchalant, but my excitement was palpable.

"By the way, what do you have me saved as in your phone?" She asked.

"Your name...why?"

Deja shook her head, disappointed. "That's boring. You've got to sell it! I have you as Wall-E in my phone."

"The robot? Why?"

"It's the only robot I could think of." She shrugged.

That pulled a laugh out of me. I reached over to grab my phone from where it rested on the center console and pulled up her contact information. She watched as I thought for a minute then typed something in the box.

"What did you change it to?" she asked, trying to peek over my hand when I put my phone back down in the center console.

"Pickles."

"Pickles?" she scoffed, "Why Pickles?"

"Because I've never seen someone order extra pickles with their burger and eat them before anything else. Pretty sure you enjoyed them more than the actual meal."

"You're the worst." She laughed. The sound was like music to my ears. "I'll see you tomorrow, Wall-E."

"Later, Pickles."

It made no sense how stuck I was on this woman already and we hadn't even kissed yet. I was trying to remain respectful of our agreement and not cross that line, but I knew that once we did, there would be no going back for me. I waited until she waved one last time and closed the door before I pulled away from her driveway, already counting down the seconds, minutes, and hours until I could see her again.

5

Deja

"Deja? Are you listening?" My client, Davian, called out for the millionth time in this zoom meeting. I blinked, embarrassed at the exasperation in his voice and tried my best to plaster on a smile.

"Absolutely. My screen just froze a bit. Keep going." We were discussing the Flirtle app. The launch date was soon, and it was time to hit the ground running with creating the buzz. My experience hadn't been great with it, but others had unparalleled success. I tried not to be bummed about not being able to find a match using the data and the code that Davian had meticulously poured over, but maybe it just meant that, much like my thoughts during this conversation, my match was elsewhere.

"Nah, I know you. Your head isn't in it. What's up? Talk to me." Davian's voice softened as he slid his glasses off his face and put them down on the desk. After working so closely together for so long, he had become more of a friend than a client.

I ran a hand down the side of my face and sighed. "I'm sorry, this wedding has taken more out of me than I thought. Is it possible for a mother to be a bridezilla when she isn't the bride or the actual mother of the bride?"

Davian laughed, "Mama Denise is intense from what you've told me. Have you found a date yet?"

My mind drifted back to Rashaad, and I fidgeted in my seat to keep from blushing. I kept replaying the night with my friends in my head. As if showing up with my favorite holiday drink in hand wasn't surprise enough, he'd picked up on my favorite color and invited me to a sacred contest with his family.

Knowing my drink and my color might be basic in the grand scheme of things, but it was the intentional effort for me. He'd made it a point to pay attention to the small details concerning me, which was something I had always done for others, but never experienced to the same degree in return. Being around someone that made it their business to learn me and anticipate what I needed felt weird in the best way possible.

The journal had been quiet this morning when I'd opened it, desperate for some clarity. I don't know what I was expecting, when I found out it was finally my turn with the magical ancient book. Maybe I wanted it to yell at me in big bold letters, HEY THIS IS YOUR MATCH! but instead, it had been subtle with the hints. Each entry offered advice that did nothing but confuse me even further.

"Yes, a-" I paused, not sure what to label him as— "friend of mine is posing as my date long enough to get my mom off my back."

"How very Hallmark movie of you."

I laughed, "Shut up. I was desperate and clearly I'm the one person on this planet that your app can't help."

Davian winced. "Again, I'm so sorry about that guy from the other night. I hate knowing a creep like that even has access."

I waved a hand, dismissing his apology. That guy was a distant memory. "It's all a part of the game. You knew there was piss in the dating pool, otherwise, you wouldn't have felt the need to create an app for it. I'm just a special case."

"So, how has the fake dating been going? Has he met your mom yet?"

"No, not yet. He's actually meeting her tonight. We're going to my parents' house for dinner. Which is why I kept zoning out. I am innately terrified that she's going to chase him away with her nice nasty, fake behavior."

"If she does, it's no sweat right? Since it's fake and you guys are just friends?" He narrowed his eyes at me. "Right?"

"Of course." I replied quickly, with a confidence I didn't quite feel. I'd be lying if I said I didn't find Rashaad extremely attractive. Whatever was bubbling between us was still new and I didn't want my mother to accidentally ruin it. It wouldn't be the first time she'd chased someone away with her well-meaning, yet very intense criticism. I didn't want that to happen this time.

After chatting a few more minutes and rescheduling the meeting for another day, when I had more brain space to focus, I logged out of the meeting and sighed loudly.

"I know that sigh." Jorja poked her head in my office. "Sounds like you need to head out early. Get your mind ready for dinner tonight."

I stood, gathering my things. "You know me well. Wish me luck."

"Luck!" she called, as I locked my office door and headed down the hall to the parking lot. One of the best things about being the boss, I didn't have to ask for permission to leave work early. Who's gonna check me?

My phone rang as soon as I reached my car. It was Brina calling me, as if she could sense I was no longer working. I smiled and slid my finger across the screen to answer the call.

"Hello, my love!" I sing-songed, starting my car.

"This wedding is going to be the death of me!" She snapped into the phone, making me laugh at the amount of frustration in her voice. We were in the final home stretch. The wedding was in two more weeks.

"We're pretty much there. You've got your dress and everything else. What are you stressing about?"

"Elodie put me in charge of communicating with the makeup artist and she has been absolutely trash at responding to my messages."

"Brin, have you been harassing that lady?" My laughter increased. Without even hearing her response, I knew my girl was probably driving the makeup artist nuts. Brina needed a set plan and she needed control. From the few conversations I'd had with the artist, I knew she was the exact opposite. Nonchalant and laid back, which could be hell for my anxious babes like Brina.

"No! I simply wanted to iron out the details for the day of, and she keeps reading my texts and not responding. I need to check this off my to-do list so I can focus on my caseload."

"Send me her number." I shook my head.

"Thank you!" she breathed, the relief evident in her tone. "How have you been lately? How's Rashaad?"

I ignored the teasing in her voice and kept my reply as short as I could. "He's fine."

"Just fine? I need more than that, Dej. We all saw the way he looked at you during the ornament making."

I made a face even though she couldn't see me. "Girl, please. He was just looking at me because I kept hogging the glitter glue."

She scoffed. "Lie to somebody else, friend. He was staring at you like you hung the moon."

I ignored the flutter in my chest at her words. He was playing the game, selling the ruse. Nothing more. It had to be believable and clearly Rashaad was a very detailed individual. It made sense that he would be aware of everyone watching us. There was nothing extra to read into. Right?

"He's coming to my parents' house with me tonight for dinner." I half whispered, half blurted.

"That's a big step." She whistled. "You nervous?"

YES! I wanted to scream, but I didn't. "Me? Nervous? Please. I don't know the meaning of the words."

Brina paused, "Your voice gets really bright and happy when

you're trying to hide how you actually feel. But I won't press you. Call me and tell me how it goes."

The call, that had taken up the small screen on my dashboard, disappeared letting me know she had hung up before I could respond. My music took over, Kehlani's soft voice filling my car. My eyes widened at how easily she called me out. I was nervous for tonight, maybe more than I even realized.

Rashaad was due to arrive at my place in less than twenty minutes. I'd just put the finishing touches on my makeup and sat down to finish my hair when the rustling from the corner of the room caught my attention.

"Finally," I muttered, rolling my eyes. This journal hadn't been very forthcoming with information the last few days and I was getting impatient. When the rustling stopped, I picked up the journal, then thought against it. I could read it later, right now I needed to focus on getting ready for this dinner. It was just my parents, but it felt monumental, like I was prepping to step into battle. A battle I wasn't sure we were equipped to win.

The doorbell ringing caught me by surprise. I still had time. I rushed past Adobe who was hopping around in circles, tail wagging a mile a minute and threw open the front door. Rashaad stood in front of me in a soft burgundy sweater and dark jeans. with his locs tied up on his head. A simple gold chain hung from his neck, complimenting the look without doing too much. My mouth watered just looking at him.

"I know I'm early." He began, oblivious. "I figured you'd want a few minutes to debrief. I know this is a big deal for you."

My heart warmed as I moved aside for him to come in. Adobe rushed him as soon as he stepped over the threshold. I opened my mouth to scold my overly excited puppy but thought against it when Rashaad bent down to scoop him up.

"My mom's whole MO is to disguise her criticism as concern and my dad considers that to be women's business and stays out of it." I finished my hair while I gave him a rundown of what to expect at dinner tonight, hoping that it would go better than I expected.

I should've known the night was going to be a mess the minute Mama opened the door.

She didn't greet me; she greeted my outfit. The dress I'd spent hours debating on wearing, the one that didn't show too much leg and covered up most of my tattoos.

"Mm," she hummed, eyes doing that slow up-and-down scan that always feels like judgment wearing pearls. "That's... festive. I suppose. Where did you get this dress from? You're so done up for a simple dinner."

I hadn't even taken my coat off yet. I guess we were starting early. "Hello to you too, Ma." I sighed, reaching in for a hug.

Rashaad stood beside me, holding a bottle of wine like a peace offering in a war zone. I watched Mama switch on her "hosting" smile, wide and bright like she was auditioning for a Christmas commercial.

"Well now," she said, tone suddenly honeyed. "You must be Rashaad. I've heard so much about you."

Have you? I wanted to ask, because I specifically remember mentioning nothing about Rashaad to her for fear of her finding a reason to cut him down. But he stepped forward, polite and warm, because he was raised right and also had no idea what sort of battlefield he'd just stepped onto.

Dinner was already plated, because Denise Johnson times food down to the second, and we took seats at the long mahogany table that always made me feel ten years old and too loud for the room.

For a while, it was fine. Or fine-adjacent. Small talk. Work talk. My dad laughed too hard at one of Rashaad's jokes. The faint jingle of the Christmas playlist Mama curated every year like it was a science, playing in the background.

And then she turned to me. Eyes bright like she was ready for a show.

"Deja, are you really going to wear your hair like that for the wedding?"

I felt my shoulders tighten. "What's wrong with my hair?" All of the bridesmaids had decided on a beautiful updo that incorporated curls and braids. We'd had the hair and makeup trial and everything looked beautiful on all of us.

"Nothing's wrong," she said, which meant everything was wrong. "It's just that some styles are, you know, more flattering. And you know how photos last forever. I'd been meaning to talk to you about it. Maybe you should consider something that frames your face a little better."

I stabbed a piece of roasted potato hard enough to nearly crack the plate. Rashaad shifted in his seat next to me. His body stiffened as if he was absorbing some of the tension that was already radiating off of me in waves.

I took a deep breath, trying to get my emotions under control. I was determined not to let her ruin my mood this early into dinner. "Ma-"

"And the bridesmaid dress," she continued, all innocent concern. "Are you sure about that fit? It's very clingy around the bust and hips. Not that you look bad. I just don't want you being uncomfortable next to all those cameras. I didn't want to say anything in front of the girls, but you should really reconsider a different style of dress. You don't want to take attention away from the bride on her special day."

"I won't," I snapped.

"And what about your tattoos? You're going to cover them, right? They're so distracting."

I could feel the anger bubbling up inside of me. "Elodie has seen every dress and every hairstyle. She's approved of all of it so there is truly no need for your concern. However misguided it might be."

"There's no need to get angry, sweetheart. I know it's a sensitive topic I'm just-"

"I wish you wouldn't," I replied, through gritted teeth.

The table went quiet. Even the Christmas music felt like it turned itself down. I felt Rashaad watching me, but I kept my eyes on my plate, willing myself not to shrink into the version of me my mother always seemed to prefer; a polished, quiet shadow.

Mama took a dainty sip of wine. "I'm only trying to help,

baby. You just get… so defensive." she sighed, as if she was so exasperated with having to correct me. Like she was doing me a favor, and I was just so ungrateful. The thing that always made me feel wrong even when I knew I was right. And before I could stop it, my throat started to sting. I needed to escape for a minute, so I could grab all of my emotions before they tumbled out of my mouth, and stuff them back down.

I grabbed my napkin and pressed it to my mouth. "I'm going to—"

"Actually," Rashaad said, placing a warm hand on my knee from under the table. His voice wasn't loud, but it cut through the room like a blade.

Mama blinked at him. "Yes, dear?"

He set down his fork gently. Too gently. Like he was controlling the urge to slam it and rolled up his sleeves to reveal the tattoos he had covering both arms. My mother's eyebrows raised, shocked at how many he had.

"I have a fair amount of artwork on my arms as well and it doesn't interfere with anything. I don't mean any disrespect," he started. "But what exactly are you helping with?" The tension in the air was so thick, you could almost see it sitting in the empty chair like a fifth person in the room. My father raised an eyebrow.

"She knows," my mother began, "She knows that I'm only looking out for her. I want what's best for my child. I want her to be comfortable."

He nodded slowly. "No, I hear you, but the way you talk to her doesn't sound like love to me. It sounds like you're telling her she's not enough. Thinly veiled criticism. And that's unfair for you to constantly pick her apart as if there was something wrong with her."

My breath caught in my throat. I vaguely registered that his hand was still on my knee, rubbing in soft calming circles.

Mama's posture went rigid. "Excuse me?"

"You keep saying you want what's best for her," he went on, calm, steady, unshakably sure. "But all I'm seeing is you picking at her. Telling her she needs to change. Highlighting every little thing like she's a flaw you're trying to fix."

I stared at him, wide-eyed. I didn't even know men like him still existed. Men who saw you. Men who said things out loud, even when the room got cold enough to form icicles.

"And Deja's not a problem to solve," he added quietly, throwing a glance in my direction. "She's incredible. As she is."

The room spun a little. Or maybe that was just me losing my grip on reality. In that moment, listening to him defend me from my own personal bully, something warm and deep bloomed in my chest.

My mother, for once, had nothing to say. She stared at Rashaad, who held her steely gaze with an icy one of his own and then looked back down at her plate. My father cleared his throat awkwardly, but I didn't miss the look on his face. He looked... impressed.

"How is the ham?" he asked, when the silence had stretched uncomfortably long.

"It's amazing." Rashaad smiled. glancing over at me again. The look in his eyes made me want to melt right there in my seat. "I'll have to get the recipe from you if you're open to sharing."

"Oh," my father chuckled. "I keep the recipe in the family only. You'll have to put a ring on that finger before I pass it to you."

Rashaad pulled his gaze away from me and settled on my father, looking like he picked up immediately on the not-so-subtle hint my father was dropping. "Bet."

It felt like my heart had dropped to my butt.

The rest of dinner, my mother and I were both quiet while Rashaad and my father carried on conversation as if they had been best friends for years. They talked football, politics, and television. Rashaad matched my father's energy word for word, bar for bar. All I could do was watch and listen in stunned silence.

My mother busied herself with clearing the table and then getting dessert together. Whenever I offered to help, she turned me down with a tight smile and a gaze that settled everywhere but on my face. Rashaad's words had connected with something in her, and she wasn't ready to speak on it at the moment. I knew I would never hear the end of it later, but for right now I wanted to bask in the peace and calm her silence provided.

"Please tell me you'll be back soon!" My father gushed. This was the most excited I'd seen him get around anyone I'd brought home. "The Broncos are playing next week."

"If you really want an audience to watch your team lose, I'll happily join you."

My dad threw his head back in good hearted laughter. "You'll be eating your words, young man."

He turned to me and scooped me up in one of those bear

hugs that used to make me feel like everything was right with the world while I was growing up. I allowed myself to relax into his embrace,

"Keep this one." he whispered in my ear and then kissed me on the cheek.

"I'll see you next week, honey," my mother said. Her eyes flickered awkwardly over to Rashaad before she smiled stiffly and waved at the two of us. I stood looking at her for a second, unsure of what to say.

"Thank you for having me," Rashaad replied, pulling me out of my trance. I followed him out to the car, still stunned and impressed.

The ride back to my place was quiet. Not awkward or tense, just charged. Like the air in the car was holding its breath right along with me. Streetlights swept through the windshield, washing Rashaad in a golden glow every few seconds. He had one hand on the wheel while the other rested on the center armrest, but his shoulders were rigid like he was waiting for my mother to materialize in the back seat and start round two.

I opened my mouth, then closed it again. I should say something, but I had no idea where to start. So many thoughts were tumbling around in my mind, all bumping into each other and making quite the mess. I wanted to thank him, I wanted to ask why he did it, I wanted to throw my arms around his neck and hug him for even feeling the need to step in on my behalf. It was something my own father hadn't bothered to do. As much as I loved my dad, I would be lying if I said that there weren't times, I wished he would step in and tell my mom to stop. I'd begun to think it just wasn't in the cards for me anymore. Until tonight.

After minutes of excruciating silence creeping by, he cleared his throat and glanced over at me. "You good?"

"I have no idea," I replied.

He nodded once and then went quiet. He didn't push or fill the silence with empty reassurance and for some reason, it made me want to take my heart out of my chest and dump it directly in his lap.

"She's always been like that."

"Does it always hit you that hard?" he asked, keeping his eyes on the road.

I hesitated. "No. Not always. I guess I'd grown used to it. When you grow up with something, you learn to name it 'love' even when it doesn't feel that way."

Rashaad let out a slow, deep breath. "You didn't deserve any of that."

"You really didn't have to say anything." My throat felt tight and I could feel my eyes start to burn. Was I really getting ready to cry in this man's car? The thug in me was disgusted at how emotional I was feeling, but it was the first time someone had witnessed my mother's criticism and felt the need to stand up for me.

"Yes. I did." His response was simple. Matter of fact.

I tried to force a laugh, but it came out more like a bark. "This fake dating situation was supposed to be easy. A few Christmas moments. Wedding vibes and then done. Light work."

"It stopped feeling like light work when I saw your face fall," he said quietly.

I turned toward the window, stunned. We pulled up to my place a few minutes later but neither one of us moved to get out. Warm air hummed through the vents as the Christmas jazz music played softly through the speakers. I smirked to myself. Of course, he would have wordless music when most people opted for the Christmas classics.

"I don't know if you expect me to apologize or not. Maybe I overstepped, but I'm not sorry."

I turned to look at him. "Not even a little?"

"No. I couldn't stomach listening to her talk to you like that. I-" He paused, then took a deep breath, "I don't like seeing you shrink. You shouldn't have to minimize any part of you for anyone. Not even her."

"Rashaad," I began, my voice shaking subtly, "why do you care so much?"

He studied my face, eyes roaming like he was trying to commit even the smallest details to memory. My body wanted to shiver under the intensity of his gaze.

"I don't know," he replied. The honesty in his voice was enough to make my chest ache. "But I do."

Fake dating wasn't supposed to feel like this. It wasn't supposed to tremble or burn or make me wonder what his mouth tastes like. It wasn't supposed to make my insides respond to him in a way that made my head spin. It was supposed to be fake. So why did everything feel too real?

He broke eye contact first, turning and hopping out of the car. I watched as he stepped around to my side, his movements confident and sure. Unlike the wild mess of emotions, I was currently feeling. He opened my door and helped me out, careful to make sure I didn't slip or fall on the ice that was steadily forming on the pavement. The snow had started when we first arrived at my parents' place and had been falling steadily ever since.

We walked to my front step, side by side. Close enough that our hands brushed, and I could feel the heat rolling off of his body in waves. He turned to me, his breath fogging the air between us, and gently warming my face. His gaze dropped to my lips for a split second, and the twinge I felt between my legs was enough to make me part my lips slightly. Hoping he would cross that line and confirm the feelings that I could no longer deny were there. But instead, he cleared his throat and stepped back.

"So, Gingerbread contest with my family tomorrow."

"Right." I breathed. "You ready?"

His eyes flashed. "I'm always ready."

"Okay," I laughed, "That got intense."

"It's a very serious event, you'll see." He grinned at me. "Goodnight, Pickles."

I rolled my eyes, trying not to smile at the stupid nickname. "Goodnight."

"Oh, and Deja?" he called. I turned back around to face him. His voice was gentle but sure. "There is nothing about you that needs to be fixed."

And when he finally walked away, leaving me standing in my doorway with my pulse racing and my face burning, I found myself already missing his presence.

"Okay, so he stood up to Mama Johnson on your behalf?" Monae repeated twenty minutes later. I'd called her as soon as I'd gotten in the house and closed the door behind me. I gave her the quick rundown of how dinner went. "Hang on, let me tag in Brina."

I waited while the line clicked over and Brina's cheerful voice piped up. "Hi, hello. I'm here for the tea. Spill. How'd it go?"

"Girl! Rashaad put Mama in her place." Monae blurted before I could answer her question. The line briefly went silent.

"What? How? Someone tell me something!" she demanded.

I rubbed my forehead. "Okay, so the dinner happened. My mom was in rare form. Like, nitpicking everything and tearing me apart in every way she could think of. And Rashaad..." I paused, still reeling. "Defended me."

"He did what?" Brina squeaked.

"Mhm! I told you! Wild!" Monae chimed in behind her.

"Yeah, he just called her out. He was calm, he was respectful, but he wasn't playing."

"How'd your mom take it?"

"Girl! She froze. Like literally clammed up for the rest of the night. I've never seen her so quiet," I replied, shaking my head.

"Aww," Brina melted.

"Oh no," Monae said at the same time. "You like him."

"I do not!" I shot back way too fast. "This is just," I waved a hand even though they can't see me, "fake. Remember? Fake dating? For the wedding? For optics or whatever?"

The line went silent. Deadly silent. I pulled the phone away from my ear to see if the call had somehow disconnected. It hadn't.

"Deja," Monae said slowly, "you never told us it was fake."

My stomach dropped to my ankles. "Oh."

"Oh?" Brina echoed. "OH?"

In my haste to deny my feelings, I blew up our spot accidentally. I groaned loudly, unsure of how to clean this one up. "Please pretend this call never happened."

"Girl, absolutely not," Brina laughed. "Because that man is not fake dating you. He is real life dating you."

Monae hummed. "And you're letting it happen."

"I am *not*—"

"Deja." Monae cut me off gently but firmly. "You should've heard how your voice changed when you talked about him. And the way he defended you? None of that sounds fake."

Brina jumped back in. "We all saw the way he stared at you like a lovesick puppy while we were making Christmas ornaments. We saw how he anticipated your needs without you having to ask or complain. He's giving 'I've loved you from the first moment I saw you' energy. He's giving 'I will stand between you and emotional trauma at your mama's dinner table.'"

I pinched the bridge of my nose. "You two are insufferable. There is no need to tag team me right now."

"And you," Monae said, I could imagine she was pointing her finger in thin air, "are in some serious trouble."

My heart thumped in my chest. "Why?"

"Because," she said like it was the simplest thing in the world, "fake or not, something real is happening."

"What does the journal say?" Brina asked, reminding me that there had been an entry that popped up right before he'd arrived to pick me up. I was in a rush at the time and hadn't stopped to read it. The new entry waited for me in my room.

"Hold that thought," I replied, sliding off the couch and heading to my room. The journal laid open where I'd left it. Untouched. I was surprised Adobe hadn't run in and turned it into his personal chew toy while I was gone. "There was an entry that popped up while I was getting ready but I didn't look at it.

"What are you waiting for?!" Brina shouted

"Girl! Stop playing and read it!" Monae said at the same time.

I rolled my eyes at their dramatics and started to read.

Dear Diary,

Tonight, something shifted in her. He saw the way her mother tried to disguise sharp words as concern, and for the first time in her life, she witnessed someone step in and demand better. He was calm and respectful, but he was unwavering. The whole room went still.

He keeps watching her in that careful and steady way that makes her feel exposed but also makes her feel safe. It wasn't part of the plan, and it definitely wasn't supposed to feel real when they agreed to this arrangement, but the warmth lingered between them long after dinner was over.

She had no idea what any of it meant yet, but something small and soft had started to shift inside of her.

6

Rashaad

I should've warned her. The thoughts kept circling through my mind as we made our way up my parents' long, brick driveway. The cold air from the heavy snow bit at my cheeks. From the outside, with all of the candy canes shoved into the grass framing the walkway and the string lights hanging from the porch, the house looked like a holiday card. But inside? Inside is war. The Gingerbread war and emotional landmines.

If Deja thought her mother was bad, she would shake in her boots at my father. Nothing I've ever done has been good enough for him. Graduated at the top of my class? He barely cracked a smile. Went in business with my friend and ended up owning one of the most successful companies in the toy making industry? Small beans. I could stand in a room and hold my own with some of the richest men and women in the world and not break a sweat but put me in a room with my dad and I was cowering in the corner like a puppy that accidentally peed on the carpet.

Deja pulled her coat tighter around her shoulders. "Okay, you're walking like a man prepping for combat. Should I be worried?"

"It's not combat," I mumbled. "More like strategic dessert engineering under an obscene amount of pressure and scrutiny."

She tilted her head. "So then, literally combat?"

"Yeah. Combat."

She laughed, low and warm, and the sound hit me square in the chest. Temporarily stilling my already buzzing nerves. As much as I loved my family, being here always managed to put me on edge, but with Deja standing next to me, it didn't feel as intense. I unlocked the front door and braced myself. All I could do was hope the feeling would last for the entire night. Maybe I'd get lucky, and we'd have a relatively uneventful competition.

"Rashaad!" My little sister, Symone, shrieked before I'd crossed a foot over the threshold. She hurtled towards me and wrapped me in a hug that nearly knocked me into the entry table. "You're late. You've missed warmups."

My sister was twenty-six years old but was living at home while she finished her PhD program. In the everyday world, she was poised and unshakeable and had her entire life together, but here? With our parents? She didn't have to lift a finger. They bankrolled her entire existence while she used her money from her well-paying job to go on trips and expand her wig collection. I was only a little irritated by the difference in treatment. She had our dad wrapped around her finger, meanwhile, he would lecture me about making too much noise if I breathed wrong around him.

"Warmups?" I repeated, dumbfounded. Every year we strayed further away from lighthearted Christmas fun and closer to a familial version of the Hunger Games.

"Of course." She rolled her eyes at me. "Winners prepare. I've been warming my wrist up for the past fifteen minutes. Who is this?" Her gaze zeroed in on Deja, who raised an eyebrow.

"I'm Deja." She smiled politely. "Nice to meet you."

"Symone," she replied dryly and turned back to me. "You've brought reinforcements."

"Reinforcements?" Deja blinked.

"You look crafty," Symone said accusingly, as if it was a crime.

"I guess so." Deja shrugged. "I'm good with my hands."

"Good? How good?"

"Symone," I hissed. "Chill. You doing too much."

Before she could protest, my mother walked in and scooped Deja up in a hug. Her graying press and curl framing her face under the Santa Hat she had strategically pinned to the top of her head. Deja leaned into the hug, which didn't surprise me. My mother had a way of making everyone feel loved with even the simplest gesture.

"You must be Deja." She pulled back to look at her. "I am Renada."

"Nice to meet you, Ms. Renada." Deja grinned. "Your outfit is absolutely everything. How'd you get the hat to stay put? I can never get it to fit over my hair."

"Oh!" My mom touched her hair absently. "I glued a headband

on the inside of it and used Bobby pins for the rest. It's a trick I learned on the Tok Tik app!"

I couldn't help but smile to myself at the way Deja got my mother to open up so quickly. I watched as she whipped out her phone and started showing some of her favorite hair influencers while Deja listened enthusiastically, pulling up the profiles on her own phone and following them.

I was just about to say something, when I felt the air in the room shift and grow colder. I glanced up to see that my father had entered the room. His glasses rested on the brim of his nose, and he stared over them at Deja and me.

He nodded at me, crisp and distant. "Son."

"Hey, dad," I replied.

His sharp gaze slid over to Deja, taking in her appearance from top to bottom. "This must be the woman that convinced my son to finally arrive on time."

I gritted my teeth.

"To be honest," Deja responded pleasantly. "He was early in picking me up, but he had to wait on me to finish my hair. Perfection takes time." She patted her braids and smiled over at my mother.

My father stared, confused. Like someone had just reported a unicorn sighting. "Well," he sniffed. "Let's get started. Shall we?"

My family truly outdid themselves this year. I was used to an intense spread, but this looked like Santa's workshop ran headfirst into a baking competition. Gingerbread panels, bowls of gumdrops, icing bags in every color, and a lazy Susan covered in candy decorated the usually pristine and stuffy dining room.

I spotted the scoreboard in the corner on an easel and groaned. Our names were written in neat loopy letters under the word 'Competitors' that had been underlined.

"Welcome to the Clairfield Family Annual Gingerbread Showdown!" Symone announced loudly, throwing her arms wide and tossing her red locs over her shoulders. My mother clapped politely while my father stood observing, like a drill sergeant.

Deja leaned forward, biting her lip to keep from smiling. "I thought you were exaggerating," she whispered.

"I would never exaggerate about something like this," I whispered back.

"The rules are simple." My father deadpanned. "You will be graded on creativity, structural integrity, and presentation. The winner-"

"Gets bragging rights until next Christmas," we all recited in tired unison. Deja looked around, amusement evident on her face.

"Begin."

We took our places at the dining room table and got to work. Deja hummed under her breath, focusing hard, with her tongue poking out slightly as she piped a swirl of icing. It was adorable and distracting. I watched her for a moment, appreciating how serious she was taking it.

My father wandered over with his hands behind his back like a disappointed auditor.

"Interesting structure," he sniffed, examining the design.

"Ambitious. As usual."

My jaw tensed.

"But ambition without correct execution..." he voice trailed off, shaking his head slightly.

There it is. The quiet disappointment. The expectation that I'd fail unless closely monitored. I don't respond, but before I could tamper down the irritation, Deja beat me to it.

"I think it's really impressive," she said, voice steady. "He's doing twice the detail I am and still helping me with mine."

My father paused.

Deja continued, gentle but firm, "And if execution is what you're worried about, there is no one more detail oriented than he is. It's almost scary how he can pick up on even the slightest imperfection."

Something inside me went very still.

My father blinked, thrown off balance. "Is that so?"

"Yes. He is a talented man." Deja shrugged as if she didn't realize the gravity of her words. "You should be proud."

The table went silent. My mom smiled at Deja knowingly, as if the two shared a secret I knew nothing about.

My father cleared his throat. "Well. Good. I've taught him well, then." And then he walked away, quieter than I'd seen him in years.

I stared at her, as she continued to build and pipe and strategically place gum drops. My hands froze and I was awestruck by this powerhouse of a woman sitting next to me.

She glanced up, catching me mid stare. "What?"

"Nothing." My voice came out rougher than I intended, which made her pause and really look at me. "Thank you."

Understanding flickered in her eyes, and she bumped her shoulder playfully against mine. "Ain't no thing." She smiled "Just returning the favor."

Symone suddenly slammed her hands on the table. "Can we get back to the competition, please?! Some of us have a reputation to uphold!"

Deja snorted and I laughed, the tension in the room lifting.

By the time the gingerbread verdict was announced, my mom pretending to be unbiased and my dad pretending he didn't already pick my sister's house before we got started, I was exhausted. I wasn't tired from the actual contest, but from the whole emotional toll being around family can cause. A few hours of trying to brace for impact can take a lot out of a person. I just wanted to go home and sit in silence for a minute.

But Deja? Deja was glowing like she was in her element. She sat on the couch laughing with my mother like she'd been coming to the house for Christmas for years. My mother had already whipped out the picture albums and was pointing to me in various stages of age and embarrassment.

Even my sister, who would usually be mentally absent and scrolling through her phone by now, was participating in the conversation. I leaned against the counter, sipping some of my mother's homemade apple cider and watched Deja work the room like it was her job.

While Deja and Symone compared Spotify playlists, my mom made her way over to where I stood. She nudged me gently with her elbow and leaned next to me. "I like her, Rashaad. She's good for you."

I coughed. "Mom-"

"She's warm. She listens. And she's not afraid to voice her opinion." She lifted brow. "You need someone like that."

Before I could respond, my dad joined us, still pretending like he didn't turn his nose up at our gingerbread house like it was a personal offense.

"Well," he folded his arms. "At least you didn't quit halfway. That's improvement. You know how you get when things get hard."

I saw Deja's shoulders tense from where she sat on the couch with Symone. When she turned to face us, her smile was polite, but there was a sharpness to it. I couldn't help but wonder if she picked that up from her mother.

"With all due respect, Mr. Clairfield, I don't think you realize how impressive your son truly is."

My father blinked, thrown off as Deja stepped closer. There's nothing confrontational about her stance, just steady fire. "Running a major company alongside Langston? Balancing operations, personnel, client management? And catching the small details Langston may miss so he can rest easy? That's not something just anyone can do."

"Especially," she continued, throwing a pointed glance at my father, "while managing impossibly high expectations. It says a lot about his resilience."

My dad cleared his throat awkwardly. "I never said he wasn't capable-"

"No." She interrupted softly. "I'm just reminding you that he is."

My mother shifted slightly, hiding the growing smile on her face. She was enjoying this way too much. Dad muttered something about checking to make sure the light fixtures were still working and wandered off to the back of the house. I exhaled, not realizing how much tension had gathered in my shoulders until I felt them drop.

Mom placed her hand over Deja's. "Thank you for that."

She shrugged like she didn't just square up to the man who scares seasoned CEOs. "He deserves to be seen."

My mother's eyes softened, and she glanced up at me. "He does."

I stood frozen in place, too scared to speak for fear of unleashing every emotion that threatened to spill out of me at once. The three women, my mom, Deja, and my sister, went back to sitting on the couch and giggling amongst themselves like nothing happened while I stood there reeling like my entire world just tilted on its axis.

I stared at the back of Deja's head, taking in the braids that she had wrapped up in an intricate bun, the earrings that dangled from her ears and the necklace that hung from her neck, and I felt myself tumbling.

I was losing my ability to decipher between what was fake and what was real between us. None of it felt fake. Every moment I spent with Deja Johnson, I wanted more, needed more. I didn't go into this arrangement expecting to fall so hard for her, but now that I was, I couldn't imagine feeling this way about anyone else.

The car ride home was quiet at first. My favorite Christmas jazz playing low. I appreciated jazz music because it could fill the space without demanding too much. Deja was curled up in the passenger seat, shoes off, with her dress draped over her legs like she was finally letting herself relax.

"You good?" I asked, glancing between her and the road,

"Your family is a lot." She leaned her head back against the seat then turned to look at me. I laughed. Understatement of the year.

"But they love you. Even if they show it in complicated ways."

I scoffed. "Complicated is generous."

She raised an eyebrow. "You know I get it. You saw my mother last night."

"You remained graceful," I said, before I could stop myself. "You handled it like a pro."

"Years of training." She snorted. "She starts criticizing and I start blocking the hits like it's a karate movie." She chopped her hands through the air playfully.

"That's what I liked about you first." I grinned, then froze, realizing what I'd just admitted.

"'First?'" she echoed, smirking.

I gripped the wheel. "Don't start."

"Oh no, I'm absolutely starting."

I breathed out a laugh and shook my head. "I just mean… you stay composed in situations most people would crumble under."

"And you stay silent," she said quietly. "Until you're pushed too far."

I swallowed. "You noticed that?"

She looked out the window, voice soft. "I notice everything."

We stopped at a red light, and she looked over at me again, really looked, like she was studying something in my expression she was trying to place.

"You know," she said, almost teasing, "your dad actually seemed impressed with me."

"He's always impressed with people who aren't his children."

"Then I guess you'll just have to borrow some of my charm next time."

"Oh, that's how it works?" I asked, raising an eyebrow at her.

She grinned. "Maybe I'll lend it to you."

The flirting was light, but the air between us wasn't. I couldn't help but zero in on the fact that she mentioned a next time. We were coming up fast on the wedding and after that, our obligations of fake dating would technically be over. There would be no 'next time'. That thought made me sadder than I expected. I wanted there to be infinite next times. I wanted her to come back with me next year. And the year after that.

"Deja?" I said, before I could think better of it.

"Yeah?"

"The way you talked about me tonight… that meant more than you know."

Her expression softened and she placed a hand on my knee. "Yeah, I know."

The light turned green, but I didn't move until a car honked behind us. She laughed as I snapped out of my trance and pressed the gas.

"It feels weird, doesn't it?" she asked, after a moment of comfortable silence. "Realizing someone finally gets it."

"Yeah, it does."

"By the way, you looked good last night when you were defending me. Very knight-in-shiny-SUV."

I laughed. "Chill."

"Nope. This is too much fun."

She had no idea how right she was.

7

Deja

"Dej! I'm dying here. I can't get the hairstylist to answer any of my calls." Monae whined into the phone. "Elodie asked me to make sure she confirmed, but at this point, the lady has fallen off the face of the planet and we're less than two weeks out."

"Text me her number." I sighed, placing the phone between my ear and shoulder so I could have both hands free.

Audrey had asked me to help with the nail tech not even a half hour earlier. So far, every task that Elodie had assigned to our friends, had been passed off to me. I didn't mind helping, but it was getting to be a bit much. I swear my phone had been ringing more in those last two hours than the entire month of November and December combined.

"You're a life saver." Monae breathed and then ended the call. My phone buzzed less than a second later with the lady's contact information. I added it to the list of things to do and sighed again. I couldn't wait for this wedding to be over, but I didn't mind taking on the extra responsibilities to make sure my girl had the wedding of her dreams.

The florist had emailed me by accident and somehow, I became looped into some emergency about ribbons. By the time the photographer texted me to confirm a start time for that day, I wanted to scream into a pillow. This was right after Jorja had called me and told me that one of my clients needed to move the meeting up because her daughter was going into labor and would deliver her first grandchild soon. Not to mention, Davian was expecting a follow up meeting to discuss Flirtle after I had been so distracted the other day.

Everybody was pulling me in a different direction, looking for me to solve the problem for them. Normally, that was no big deal. I thrived in moments like this, but every now and then, the tasks began to pile up. It took everything in me not to cancel everybody and tell Elodie to take Mekhi to the nearest courthouse and elope.

I love my girls. Truly. They're my whole heart, but being the unofficial fixer of the group was cute in college when the biggest problem was a missing phone charger or needing to borrow a lip gloss. Now I was stuck coordinating so many extra parts of this wedding so we could shield Elodie from added stress. The weight of it was hitting me square in the chest.

My phone buzzed again, but this time with a text from Rashaad.

You good, Pickles? Haven't heard from you today.

On any other occasion, this text would have brought a smile to my face but right now it just felt like another added thing tugging at me. Another person expecting something from me. I typed a hurried response and then pressed send, thinking of the millions of things I needed to get done before the day ended.

I'm fine. Just busy. Not important. I'll talk to you later.

As soon as I put my phone down, regret immediately took over. That text was too snappy and dismissive. He didn't deserve that. All he was doing was checking in. That was not how we usually spoke to each other. I waited for the text bubbles to pop up, something to let me know that he wasn't upset. He read the message, but no response came.

A familiar buzzing panic started in my ribs. Everything felt too fast, too tight, too loud, too much. I tried to breathe but it came out shallow and choppy. My vision began to pinch and blur around the edges.

It'd been a while since I had a panic attack. Usually, I was pretty good about delegating when my plate began to get a little too full, but this had caught me off guard. I sank on to the couch, gripping the phone like it was my one and only lifeline. Why did everything feel like too much today? And why was it making me feel so much worse that Rashaad didn't bother to text back?

It'd been an hour, and the panic had not subsided long enough for me to start tackling things on the list. I pressed a hand to my chest, trying to steady my heart and focus on my breathing. In through the nose, out through the mouth. I've talked so many people down from a panic attack in my lifetime, but now that it was my turn, I had nothing. No advice to give myself. No words of wisdom or affirmations to chant until it stopped feeling like I was trying to run a marathon with a teenager on my back. Adobe licked my hand and nudged his way into my lap. I allowed him to comfort me in the best way he could, while the overwhelmed tears fell down my face.

I couldn't do this. It was too much. I'd have to call my girls back and tell them that I couldn't save the day this time. I opened my phone, scrolling through the numbers, when a soft knock hit my door. I froze.

"Deja, it's me." Another knock; firmer this time. "Open the door."

My heart thumped so hard, I could feel it in my teeth. I jumped up, hastily wiping the tears from my eyes and threw open the front door. Rashaad stood there in a black hoodie and jeans, his locs in two-barrel twists, holding a grocery bag. His expression was stubborn; the same look I saw on his face when he marched into my office and suggested we fake date.

"Wh-What are you doing here?" I stuttered, my voice cracking like thin shards of glass.

He stepped inside without waiting for the invite and closed the door behind him. He took a look at me in my stained sweatpants, too big t-shirt, messy hair, and held up the bag.

"When I get stressed, I snack. So, I brought the essentials," he said. "Salt and vinegar chips, Talenti coffee chocolate chip gelato, soft baked fudge cookies, and that peach tea that I think is gross, but you can't seem to get enough of."

My throat tightened, tears threatening to start again. "Rashaad..."

He set the bags on the counter and then turned to me, studying my expression. "You sounded off. I figured the wedding stuff was getting stressful and you needed help, but your stubborn ass wasn't going to ask for it."

"I'm fine," I replied weakly.

"You're lying."

That broke something in me and the tears began to flow, blurring my vision, and making me sniff. "I'm doing the best I can," I wailed. "I'm trying so hard to keep everything together for everyone and today is just-" I took a quick gasp of air. "Today it just piled up."

"Okay," he replied, taking a small step towards me and placing his hands on my shoulders. "Let me carry some of it."

I blinked. "Why?"

"Everybody needs help sometimes." He placed a finger under my chin and tilted my face towards his. "And besides, what kind of man would I be if you cried out for help and I ignored it?"

"But I didn't," I shot back. "I didn't say anything."

"I still heard it." He grinned. "Now, you drink some of that disgusting tea and tell me what you need to get done today."

"I'm fine." I tried again. "I don't need-"

"Deja," he replied sternly. "Don't piss me off."

"Alright, alright." I pointed a thumb at my open computer on the counter. "My Excel sheet is in there. Everything that needs to be done today is in red."

He stepped around me and peered at the screen. I watched as he quietly read the list, eyebrow arching higher than I'd ever seen it. "This list is mostly red."

"Exactly."

"No sweat. Let's get to it."

Three hours, and two angry conversations about final nail designs later, Rashaad had contacted each one of the wedding vendors and confirmed appointments with the photographers while I was able to catch up on my work for the day.

I kept shooting glances in his direction as he paced in the middle of my floor arguing back and forth with the florist about whatever ribbon crisis she had been emailing me about. After everything finished, we ordered a pizza, and he flopped on my couch next to me.

"Wedding planning is no joke." He sighed. "I see why the bride is usually so stressed out."

I laughed. "Yeah, we agreed to try and take as much stress off her plate as we could."

"We? Seems like you were doing a lot of the work there."

"My girls have been pretty busy lately. Brina has taken on extra caseload, Monae has been covering extra shifts at the fire station, and this is Audrey's busy season at the restaurant. I don't mind stepping in for my girls." I shrugged, biting into a slice of pepperoni pizza. The gooey cheese and salty pepperoni felt like the right source of comfort after an emotionally taxing day.

He nodded, taking a bite of his own slice. "You took on a lot of extra stress."

"Don't think this means I can't handle the marketing for Brain Box. I don't usually have panic attacks in the middle of my work week."

"Relax, Pickles. Everybody has bad days. Do you think I'm on my A-game all the time?"

I shrugged. "Yes, actually. You are a robot, after all."

"Even robots get overwhelmed sometimes." He rolled his eyes at my joke attempt. "I'm just saying, you don't have to try and explain away a bad day. We all have them."

We ate in comfortable silence. His presence grounding me after starting the day feeling like I was going to float away in a bubble of panic. Rashaad has seen everything I've tried to hide. The overwhelm, the pressure, and the way I tend to take on too much without blinking. He sensed the panic I didn't know how to articulate and he came without me having to ask.

"What's that noise?" he asked, tilting his head to the side. Sure enough, the soft rustling from my bedroom carried into the living room. I wiped my hands on a napkin and stood up.

"I think I left the window open in my room; I like to sleep cold." I lied, "I'll be right back."

I hurried into my bedroom just in time to see the pages in the journal stop flipping. So far, the entries hadn't been exactly what I was hoping for when Monae told me it was my turn. I had been hoping for the bright neon signs telling me exactly who my man was. Was it Rashaad? Did he feel the same way about me? Or was it someone else I hadn't met yet? Instead, each message referred to my man as "he" and left little clues for me to figure out who it was talking about.

As if I didn't already have enough on my plate, I was expected to decipher this magical phenomenon as well. I reached for it, hoping that this time the clue would be more obvious.

"Come on, explain this to me like I'm five." I grumbled, looking down at the words on the page.

Dear Diary,

There are some storms a person hides so well that even they forget they're standing in the rain. Yet, the right ones will notice. Without words, without clues, and without being asked.

He stepped in, not to rescue her, but to remind her that she was never meant to carry the world on her own. The one that is specifically meant for her will always sense the shift in breath, the hitch in her voice, and will always see the weight she tries to sparkle over.

"This has to be about Rashaad, right?" I mumbled to myself. Who else would it be about? He was the one that had sensed I needed him and swooped in to save the day. It wasn't like I had a ton of men lined up at my door waiting to anticipate my every need.

"Aye, Pickles! Did you fall out the window or something?"

Rashaad called, his voice muffled as he talked around his next pizza slice. With the way that man could eat, if I waited too long, there wouldn't be much left.

"Very funny," I called back, closing the journal and leaving it on my bed. I would figure out what to make of it later.

8

Deja

Dear Diary,

What began as protection has blossomed into possibility and the next choice they make will shape everything that follows. The heart she fears showing is the very one he is meant to see, but if she hesitates now, the moment may slip into silence. Silence can be mistaken for indifference.

One path opens if she speaks. Another if she doesn't.

I tossed the journal to the side, frustrated. None of the entries gave me any comfort or told me how Rashaad was feeling. The cryptic messages were getting harder and harder to interpret. It had given my friends much more obvious advice when they were sorting through their love lives, yet it waited until it was my turn to act like it didn't want to work anymore.

Adobe nuzzled his nose into my leg and looked up at me. Those round, doe eyes making me sink to the floor to pet him.

"Not right now, baby. Mommy has to go out for a bit." I scratched him behind the ears. "But as soon as I come back, you and I will snuggle and watch The Grinch."

I grabbed my keys from the kitchen counter and headed out. When I slid into the booth across from Rashaad, my stomach was already a jumble of nerves. Elodie sent a text to the group begging us to do this last-minute bridal party Christmas activity before the wedding kicks up at the end of the week. The local market was having a Christmas expo. Vendors booths of all types would be available for cute holiday themed crafts and gifts.

We'd all, somewhat reluctantly, agreed to meet up there that evening. Immediately after, Rashaad had texted me separately, with a cryptic message asking if we could meet up for coffee before we went. I tried to probe for answers on what he needed to so urgently discuss in person, but he wouldn't give me anything. As I sat across from him in the booth, while he pretended to study the menu, my mind raced.

"So," he began, not looking up from the menu. "I feel like we need to discuss what this is."

"This is a coffee shop," I replied, purposely ignoring what I knew he meant. "What you're holding is called a menu."

He gave me that patient look he gave when he knew I was being dramatic on purpose, before leaning back in the booth. His eyes looked tired, like he had been tossing and turning all night. I wanted to ask but it didn't feel right to do in this moment.

"Deja."

"Rashaad," I echoed.

"This is starting to feel a bit too real for me." He sighed, running a hand over his face.

"Oh," I replied. My insides began to scramble, panic settled on my shoulders like a warm blanket in an already warm room and before I could stop myself, I was brushing it off with a joke. "Not sure why. It's strictly platonic. Not my fault if you fell in love with me. I am amazing, after all."

He exhaled, half laugh and half surrender and then stared at me. I held his gaze for as long as I could before I got uncomfortable and had to look away. It felt like he was looking into my soul and if he looked hard enough, he would see the version of me whose feelings had just gotten hurt.

"So, this hasn't felt like...more to you?" he asked, leaning down to catch my eye again. Instead, I picked up the menu and held it in front of my face so he couldn't see how much this conversation was getting to me.

"Not at all. If anything, you got a little sentimental at my parents' house first. Defending me to my mother? Bold move, Clairfield."

He rubbed the back of his neck. "Yeah well, someone needed to."

"It didn't have to be you," I replied, a little more forcefully than I'd intended.

"I just did what felt natural."

"Well," I said, folding my arms, "since we're clarifying things, let me clarify something too: I have no feelings for you. This is strictly a platonic partnership, and I have no intentions of taking this any further once this wedding is over."

He sat back, looking like someone had punched him in the gut. "I mean, I'm on what you're on. So, if that's what you want, then cool."

"Cool," I replied. Even though it didn't feel cool at all. Looking at the expression on his face, the closed off emotionless version of him that I'd originally met, I couldn't help but wonder if I misread. Maybe this conversation wasn't going to go the way I'd assumed and, in my rush to beat him to the punch, I went too far.

It was too late to take it back now. If there was one thing about me, it was that I stood on business. So, I'd have to follow through, even if the idea of no longer having him around made me sadder than I expected.

The snow dusted market looked like it was straight out of a Christmas movie. It was warm, golden, and impossibly magical. The wooden vendor stalls lined the cobblestone path; their roofs heavy with snow and the edges trimmed in thick garland. A glowing snowflake lantern hung from each stall, slowly swaying in the breeze.

Every vendor booth was overflowing with treats; jars of candied nuts, sugared pastries, peppermint bark next to the christmas cookies and the tiny, wrapped gifts tied with swine. Lights spiraled up the trees and Christmas music hummed faintly from a speaker tucked behind the garland. The blend of music with the soft crunch of the snow under our feet was the perfect combination to really put you in the holiday spirit.

But I was too in my head to enjoy it.

I stood beside Rashaad, tall, warm, and gray peacoat fitting him unfairly well, with the wind biting at my face and my heart trying to thump its way through my ribs. I kept stealing glances at him when he wasn't looking and mentally kicking myself for not pushing past the awkwardness of our earlier conversation and telling him how I truly felt.

On my millionth glance in his direction, he was already watching me.

"You're quiet. You good?" He bumped his shoulder against mine.

"I can be quiet," I snapped.

His eyes twinkled with amusement. "I didn't say you couldn't. It's rare though."

Before I could flip him off, the wind blew harder, making me shiver involuntarily. My coat, even though it was one of my thicker ones, felt thin in the bitter cold. Rashaad wordlessly pulled off the scarf that was looped around his neck and wrapped it around my shoulders. It smelled just like him, cognac with a bit of vanilla and sandalwood.

"That better?" he asked. I nodded, unable to think of anything to say in the moment.

"It's freezing out here!" Audrey complained as she walked up tugging Montrell behind her. He wrapped his arms around her and nuzzled his nose into her neck. I watched for a moment, pretending like I wasn't wishing Rashaad was doing that to me and then turned to find him staring directly at me. That same piercing gaze that saw way too deeply into my mind. Studying me like I was his favorite subject in school.

"Why do you keep staring at me?" I asked, through gritted teeth. "It's getting creepy, Clairfield."

"Sorry." He shrugged. "I'm going to look around for a bit. You good here?"

My heart sank, but I forced a smile and nodded. "Sure!"

He nodded and then stalked off in the distance. I watched him for a moment, debating whether I should swallow my pride and tell him that I was wrong. Instead, I turned, just as Elodie, Brina, and Monae walked up. I schooled my features into a cheerful smile and waved.

"Where are the guys?" I asked as I leaned in to hug each one of them.

"They wandered off somewhere." Elodie grinned, her cheeks flushed red in the cold.

"How are you doing?"

"I'm good, even though it's freezing out here." As if on cue, my body shuddered involuntarily. "We're only a few days out, lady! How are you feeling?"

"More than ready to call that man my husband!" Elodie's grin spread as she clapped her hands. I was so happy for my girl. The family she found in Mekhi and Kellan was something for the storybooks. It was hard to believe that the little boy those two fell in love with during an emergency foster situation, was now gearing up to go to college on a music scholarship.

My mind drifted back to the journal that was sitting on my bed open to the last entry. That same journal had led all four of my friends to the love of their lives, but for some reason, it felt like it was doing the opposite for me. Maybe it was broken. After dealing with all of my hard-headed friends, maybe there wasn't enough magic left for me. Maybe that just meant I needed to make my own.

"Where's Rashaad?" Monae asked, looking around.

I spotted him over by the vendor with a bunch of ornaments. While he studied her collection, the lady running the booth was too busy studying him. Anger swelled in my belly as I watched him mention something to her that made her throw her head back and laugh. My vision began to blur at the corners when she reached out and touched his arm.

He wasn't that funny. There was no need for all that extra. I wanted to march over there and demand to know what was so funny, but I didn't. It wasn't my place. After all, I just told this man that I had no interest in him and just wanted to keep this ruse platonic. He was well within his right to entertain this ogre if he wanted to do so.

"He's over there looking at ornaments." I replied stiffly. The girls followed my gaze, while I busied myself with checking out the pastries at the table we stood in front of. "Doesn't this look yummy?"

"Okay, what's going on?" Elodie asked, narrowing her eyes at me.

"Nothing."

"They're 'fake dating' even though none of it seems very fake."

Monae blurted. Audrey and Elodie exchanged a glance and then yanked me by the arm of my coat.

"Hey!" I whined.

"What is she talking about?" Elodie demanded.

"You wanted us to have dates to the wedding." I shrugged. When Elodie folded her arms and glared at me, I cracked and explained the entire charade. I told her how I'd made the agreement with Rashaad in order to keep her happy and keep my mother off my back just long enough to get through the wedding.

"Only, real feelings have started to develop." Brina finished for me. I glared at her but said nothing. I couldn't deny it. Not anymore.

"I told him that this was just a ruse, that I had no intentions of continuing once the wedding was over." I groaned, running a mittened hand down my face.

"Now, why the hell would you do something stupid like that, girl?" Monae asked, folding her arms. All of them stared at me like I'd lost my mind.

"Because he said it was starting to feel too real and I panicked!"

Brina shrugged. "That doesn't mean he was going to back out of it though."

"I'm aware of that, but you try imparting logic when your brain is in anxiety overload!"

I sighed loudly, feeling even worse about the impulsive decision I had made. Elodie's expression softened and she placed her hands on my shoulders.

"What do you want to happen, Dej?"

"I want this snow to melt for one thing and then-"

"Deja." She interrupted.

I sighed. "Fine. I want him. This stopped being fake for me a while ago. Being with him feels...right. And I think I might have messed it up." A single tear slipped down my cheek as I pointed to where Rashaad stood talking with the lady at the ornament stand.

"Girl, please." Monae scoffed. "That girl has nothing on you."

"Even if this started off as some type of ruse between you two," Elodie began, wiping the tears that had started to fall from my eyes, "I don't think that's what it is now. We've all seen the way he looks at you."

"He hasn't stopped wearing burgundy since he realized it was your favorite color." Brina chimed in. "Langston told me that he went out and bought more sweaters in that shade."

"Really?" I sniffed. I had noticed that he'd been wearing it more often, but I just assumed he liked the color the same way I did. I wiped my eyes and smiled. "The thug in me is disgusted at these tears."

All five of us giggled. I sniffled, shaking my head at the tangle of emotions I didn't expect to come pouring out of me. That wasn't something I typically allowed to happen in public, but being open and honest with my girls made me feel so much better than I expected.

"We've all shed a thug tear or two when it was our turn and you were there to be the voice of reason for each of us." Audrey grabbed my hand and squeezed it gently. "We are living our love stories in real time."

"It's about time you lived yours."

9

Rashaad

The second I looked up and saw Langston striding through the crowd, eyes narrowed, I knew I was about to get an earful. When he reached me, he didn't even bother with a greeting, just folded his arms and glared at me like I'd done something to personally offend him.

"So, fake dating, hmm?" He tilted his head to where Deja was talking with her friends in hushed tones. I watched them for a minute then dragged my gaze back to him. "Looks real fake to me."

I gritted my teeth. "Langston, don't start."

"Ain't nobody starting. I'm just observing." He folded his arms. "You've been out here buying burgundy colored everything since you found out she likes it. I see the way you stare at her whenever she's not paying attention. You down bad. Admit it."

I scrubbed a hand down my face. "It's not even like that."

Langston raised an eyebrow; the same look he gave me when I told him I was taking Deja to the gingerbread competition at my parents' house "You sure?"

"Positive." The lie tasted bitter. "She decided she just wanted to be friends."

Langston's head jerked toward me so fast I'm surprised he didn't pull something. "Friends?"

"Yeah." I shifted my weight, suddenly very interested in the Christmas tree shaped treat samples at the nearby booth. "We talked. And she said it, clear as day. Platonic. Strictly for the ruse."

"And that's what you want?" Langston asked, his voice low, his expression softened.

I swallowed hard. "No."

The word felt like it'd been sitting in my chest all day, heavy and hot. Langston sighed like he'd been waiting for me to stop lying to myself and admit that. "So why didn't you say something?"

"I tried," I said quietly, watching Deja laugh at something Elodie said. She looked happy. Light in a way I hadn't seen before. Light in a way I wanted to protect. "At the coffee shop. I told her that this was starting to feel too real. I was trying to get the words out. I was nervous as hell, but I was trying."

Langston looked genuinely confused. "And?"

"And before I could say anything, she nodded like she solved an equation. She was like, 'I have no feelings for you. This is strictly a platonic partnership, and I have no intentions of taking this any further once this wedding is over.'" I pushed out a breath. "And I froze."

Langston stared at me. "You? Freeze? You neva freeze!"

"Not the time for Black Panther quotes," I snapped. "She caught me off guard. I thought that's what she wanted. And I…" I glanced away. "I didn't want to pressure her."

Langston's expression softened. "You weren't pressuring her, man. You were catching feelings."

I winced. "Don't say it like that."

"I will say it like that. Because it's true." He nudged my shoulder. "Rashaad, I've known you for years. I've seen you date, I've seen you 'not date,' I've seen you run like your life depended on it anytime a woman so much as mentioned her five-year plan." He tilted his head. "But I've never seen you look at someone the way you look at Deja."

"She scares the hell out of me," I admitted, finally.

Langston snorted. "Remember how I told you I couldn't wait for the day a woman knocked you on your ass? Welcome to love, my friend."

"I didn't say love."

"You didn't have to." He grinned. "Your face said it for you. It's real pitiful."

I groaned. "You're insufferable."

"And you're in denial." He clapped my shoulder. "Look, man. If you want her, like actually want her, you'll have to say it. Out loud. To her. Not to me. Not to the peppermint bark lady. To her."

"She made up her mind," I said quietly.

"Then un-make it." Langston shrugged. "Unless you're really okay being just her 'fake date.'"

I was not. I absolutely was not. Because somewhere between the fake smiles and the made-up backstory and the Christmas events, something real started. Something I didn't want to lose.

Langston followed my gaze and smirked. "Go get your girl."

"She's not my girl."

"Not yet," he said, "But if you keep stalling, someone will swoop in without hesitation." I glared at him as he faked dropping the mic and walked off like he just declared prophecy. After he disappeared into the crowd like some smug Christmas angel sent to ruin my mood, I stole one more glance at Deja across the market. Her friends were surrounding her, talking about something. She was bundled in that deep green coat that made her look like wrapped luxury.

I needed a second to breathe. I needed a minute to think and stop pretending that I was okay with being just a friend. I drifted further down the rows of vendors where the ornament booths sparkled. One display immediately grabbed my attention, not because it was beautiful, but because it was offensively ugly. Glittery, neon-green, and bumpy shaped like a pickle. A whole wall of them, hung proudly like they were masterpieces and not a hazard to interior design.

I snorted to myself and then froze.

Of course, this is the one that felt like it was staring at me.

My mind flashed back to the day we'd met for lunch, after she had a rough dress fitting with her mother. She'd ordered extra pickles. A ton of them. Enough to make the waiter pause to clarify if they'd heard her correctly. That was the same night I'd changed her name to Pickles in my phone. The way she rolled her eyes at me made me smile like a loser because her irritation was adorable. She said it was a terrible name, but she didn't make me change it.

I stood in front of this glittery pickle ornament, bright and unapologetically ridiculous, and it felt like fate was wagging its finger in my face. The vendor, a woman with long hair and round glasses drifted over.

"Looks like you found a good one."

I knew she was talking about the ornament, but my mind still drifted back to Deja. Her laugh, the way she made a joke when she was trying to hide her real feelings, the way she stepped into my chaotic family and smoothed it over like it was an easy project. The way my chest ached whenever she wasn't around. Or when I glanced at my phone every few seconds, hoping to see a text message from her. How she understood me without me having to explain much of anything.

"I did," I whispered.

The vendor cleared her throat gently. "Would you like me to wrap it for you, sweetie?"

I nodded, voice caught in my throat. "Yeah. It's hideous, but I'll take it."

She threw her head back and laughed. "It is. But people like it that way." She carefully placed the glitter pickle in a tiny red box and handed it to me with a knowing smile; her hand rested on my arm. "I think she'll love it."

"I hope so," I whispered.

This felt like more than just an ornament. It was me finally admitting that I didn't want this to end. Not after Christmas. Not ever. I wanted her for as long as she'd have me. I tucked the box in my coat jacket and headed back over to where Deja stood with her friends.

The little red box felt like it weighed five hundred pounds in my pocket. It kept tapping against my chest with every step I took through the market. Like a little reminder not to punk out. The second our eyes connected, my heart stuttered.

"Hey," I said quietly.

"Hi," she replied, smiling up at me. "You disappeared. I'd thought maybe you got abducted by the kettle corn people."

"Would you have rescued me?"

"Probably not," she deadpanned. "They had free samples."

I choked out a laugh, the joke hit me right in the ribs. The ease between us that hasn't existed with anyone else, I could live in it forever and never come up for air. Her friends all wandered off, one by one, with their dates in tow leaving us in this quiet moment alone. She nudged my arm with her shoulder.

"Buy anything?"

My fingers brushed across the box in my jacket before I could stop myself. Not yet. It's not time yet.

"Just shopping." I tried to sound casual, but I failed. "Just grabbed something I realized I needed."

"Oh?" she asked, amusement slipping into her voice. "For the wedding? Or for Christmas? Or—" her eyes narrowed suspiciously, "—is it food? Because you look like a man who bought secret snacks. And if you did, I demand that you share."

"No." I laughed. "Not snacks."

Snowflakes stuck to her lashes as she looked up at me, and suddenly the moment felt warm, even though we were standing outside in the cold air. I almost reached for the ornament in my coat. I almost got down on one knee and presented it like I was proposing, but I didn't. She shivered and the moment popped. I couldn't give it to her right now. Not yet.

But I would.

Soon.

By the time we pulled up to her house a few hours later, my nerves were completely shot. I spent the entire rest of the night and the car ride over debating, should I pull over and give it to her, wait until after the wedding, or bury it in the drawer and pretend like I never had any feelings for her to begin with. Like a rational adult.

I was still debating when she unbuckled her seatbelt and offered a tiny smile. The one that I could feel in my chest, every single time.

"Tonight was fun. Very platonic." There went that word again. I didn't respond, the words getting stuck in my throat. I watched, panicked, as she reached for the door handle and that's when I knew. I couldn't let the night end without telling her how I felt.

"Deja, wait."

She paused and then turned back to me. The expression on her face was unreadable. I cleared my throat awkwardly and reached into my coat. My fingers curled around the tiny box, and I took a deep breath.

"I got you something."

Her eyebrows lifted as I handed her the box. My hands were steady on the outside but on the inside, I was a mess. She opened it slowly, the tissue paper fluttering under the heat blowing from the vents. When the ornament appeared, she froze for a split second before her hand flew to her mouth, a laugh bubbling before she could clamp it down.

"Rashaad you did not!"

"I did."

She lifted it gently, the glitter shimmering under the dim light of the streetlamp. It's gaudy. It's ridiculous. But it was perfect.

"An ugly pickle."

"'An ugly pickle,'" I echoed. My voice was lower than I intended.

Her eyes flickered up to me. "Why?"

I tried to explain, but the words got tangled somewhere between my brain and my mouth. Because I laughed for ten solid minutes when you ordered enough pickles to make the waiter judge you. Because it's your contact name in my phone. Because I wanted you to think of me every time you passed by your tree. But before I could say any of that, I could see the realization settle over her face.

"You chose this because it's ours," she whispered.

My breath hitched. "Yeah."

Her fingers brushed the ornament, then curled around it. She looked unsteady in a way I'd never seen before.

"It's perfect." she said.

I leaned forward, not close enough to kiss her, just enough that I could and paused, giving her the option to take it further. Without hesitation, she closed the distance between us and pressed her lips against mine. It was soft at first, but then it grew more frantic, more desperate. I pushed my seat back and in one smooth motion, she'd unbuckled her seatbelt and threw her leg over me.

The heater hummed and music played softly in the background as our tongues danced together in a mix of passion and intimacy. I had been waiting for this moment, dreaming about what it would be like, wondering how she would taste and how she would feel in my arms.

It was better than anything I could have ever imagined. Little whimpers escaped her as our kisses deepened. She fit perfectly in my lap, like she had always been meant to be there. I was losing myself in the kiss, getting dizzy with desire when she pulled back to look at me.

"I don't want it to end." She breathed.

I laughed. "I don't either."

"I want you to come with me to all of my family dinners and Christmas parties." She planted little kisses on my lips between each word.

"I want that too."

"Do you want to come inside?" she asked.

I bit my lip, "If I go in there, I don't know if I'll be able to control myself," I admitted.

"Good. Don't."

I leaned back to look at her. Her eyes were low and her lips were puffy and her hands rubbed my chest in small comforting circles. I knew, just by looking at her, that I was getting ready to meet a side of Deja that I had never seen before.

"Lead the way."

10

Deja

"I cannot believe my wedding day is tomorrow!" Elodie sighed. "I feel like I'm going to throw up." She fanned herself dramatically.

"You pregnant?" I asked, wiggling my eyebrows and then ducked, laughing, as a pillow flew at my head. "I'm just checking!"

We were all gathered in the hotel next door to the library where the wedding would be held, getting ready for the rehearsal dinner. As excited as I was to see Elodie and Mekhi officially get hitched, I was mostly relieved that the wedding itself was finally coming to an end. I slipped into my dress, a gold bodycon dress that fell low on my shoulders and had just started my makeup when there was a knock on the suite door.

"I got it. It's probably Kellan coming to ask what suite the men are getting ready in." Audrey turned and headed for the door. "Oh. Hi."

"Is my daughter here?" My mother's voice traveled through the room. My body went stiff for a second, before I sighed and forced myself to relax. I hadn't talked to her since dinner when Rashaad had called her out on the way she constantly criticized me. I could only imagine what extra drama she had cooked up in the few days of silence.

"Hey, ma." I smiled, stepping out of the bedroom of the suite and into the living room area. She looked expensive in her navy-blue sheath dress and gold heels. "You look beautiful."

She smiled, "Thank you. Listen, I wanted to talk to you before the excitement of the weekend really starts." I watched, confused as she fidgeted with her fingers, looking everywhere but at me. She seemed...nervous and that was very unlike her.

"Is everything okay?"

"Honestly, no." She sighed. Panic began to bubble; I curled my toes in my slippers and pressed them against the floor as a way to ground myself. "I wanted to apologize."

I blanched. "Huh? You what?"

"I want to apologize," she repeated. "I've been thinking about the conversation with Rashaad the other night and I realized that he was correct. I am too critical of you."

I stayed silent, stunned.

"It's not because I'm not extremely proud of you because I am. Deja, baby, I am so beyond proud of you. But if I'm honest, you've always scared me."

I felt something in my chest loosen and tighten at the same time. "What do you mean?"

"With the way I grew up, you had to be a certain way to be accepted in society. You had to look a certain way, act a certain way, no hair out of place, don't draw attention to yourself. That is what I tried to instill in you because that's what I knew. That's how I survived." She took a cautious step closer, placing her hands on my shoulders and smiling wistfully at me.

"You fought so hard against that," she continued "and the harder you fought against it, the more scared I became because I didn't think I had anything of value to teach you. I didn't know how to help you. Or be there for you. Or protect you from this world."

"I don't need you to protect me," I whispered. "I just needed you to love me."

"I know that now. You needed encouragement and acceptance. Not constant criticism. I didn't see that in my desperation to protect you; I was actually hurting you." My mother swallowed hard, her eyes welling with tears. Seeing her so emotional hit me in the chest.

"Mama..." I choked out, my throat tight. "You've never apologized like this before."

"I know." She smiled sadly. "I'm trying to do better. To be better. For you."

I didn't trust my voice, so I just stood there, breathing around the ache in my chest. She reached out, brushing my cheek the way she used to when I was little. "I want to fix this. Our relationship. If you'll let me."

Something inside me cracked open, not in a painful way, but in a way that let light in the darker parts of my heart. The parts that

I had come to accept would never be fixed. Until now.

"I'd like that," I said softly. "I really would."

She nodded, eyes shiny. "Good." Then she added, with a tiny laugh, "That young man of yours is… honest. And protective. I can see why you care for him."

My mind drifted back to Rashaad, after finally admitting that we liked each other, we hadn't been able to keep our hands to ourselves. I smiled, knowing that I was finally experiencing the love I'd seen my friends have.

I laughed, "Who knew all it'd take would be for him to call you out on your mess."

My mother laughed with me, wiping her eyes quickly. "You look beautiful, by the way."

I did a little twirl, showing her the dress from different angles. She nodded approvingly and then gave me another hug. "We'll talk after this weekend. I want to take you to lunch."

"Only if you're paying."

She tapped me on the nose with a smile and then headed out of the suite. I stood where I was for a moment, taking in the fact that a dynamic I had given up hope on, was finally starting to turn in a different direction.

I should have been focused on the chicken parmesan. It was honestly delicious, but my mind was still reeling from the earlier conversation with my mom. After she left, I'd rushed back into the bedroom where my girls were pretending they weren't eavesdropping, and allowed myself one minute to cry before getting back to business. I could focus on it once the weekend was over.

I glanced down at the table, taking in the sight of my four favorite women and their dates. Elodie's bridal glow was so blinding that the food barely registered. Brina and Langston were whispering about something, Audrey was reciting her maid of honor speech under her breath, and Monae was trying to pretend that she wasn't crying every time she looked over at Elodie and Mekhi.

Just as I was reaching for another piece of garlic bread that I absolutely did not need, Elodie's grandmother, Amada, stood up. She had been observing quietly, with a faint smile on her face. Birdie Mae, her best friend, sat at the table next to her. The two of them together radiated grace and elegance in a way that I could only hope for when I reached that age.

She gently tapped her fork on her glass, and the room fell silent in seconds. Everyone in the room could sense in her stance and in her energy that she was about to say something important, and no one wanted to miss it.

"Before we head into the wedding tomorrow," she began, tucking a stray silver curl back into the bun at the nape of her neck. "I think it's time I finally tell you all of the truth. Especially you girls."

My heart hiccupped as she turned her steady gaze on the five of us. Elodie was already smiling like she knew exactly what her grandmother was about to say. Brina clasped her hands, and Monae perked up, dabbing at her wet eyes with the corner of her napkin.

She held up the journal that she'd asked me to make sure I brought with me and smiled.

"This journal has had quite the journey," she said. "It was given to me by my grandmother, but it didn't begin with her. It goes much, much farther back than that."

Everyone leaned in. Birdie Mae was the only one who didn't look surprised by anything Amada was saying.

"The journal was owned by a man named Saint Nicholas."

I choked on my water. "Like...Santa? The Santa Claus?" I whispered to Monae.

"Shhh!" She hissed.

Amada smiled, like she'd heard me. "Not the storybook version. The real Nicholas, before legends whitewashed him and wrapped him in velvet. He was a wealthy man with eight brothers. Dasher, Dancer, Prancer, Vixen, Comet-" She waved her hand, "You get the idea. Anyway, he had always been a generous man and would do whatever he could to make sure his community was without need." Silence stretched across the room as she spoke, even the wait staff had stopped to listen to the story she told.

"Every year around this time, he and his brothers would travel to each house in their small neighborhood and ask what was one special gift that they wanted. He arrived at the house of a man with three daughters who owed a debt he could not pay. As punishment, they were going to take his three daughters and sell them into slavery to erase the debt. Nicholas secretly paid the dowries so each daughter could be free to choose her own path. The eldest daughter gave him this journal as a thank you." She held it up again, and suddenly the old book seemed so much more powerful than it had before. Like it glowed under the light.

"She told him that the journal would bring him what he desired most." Amada continued, pausing to look at each one of us, "And Nicholas, despite everything he had and all of his giving, was incredibly lonely. His one desire left unfulfilled was love."

"Oh my god," Brina whispered.

"The eldest daughter told him that the next year, as a thank you for all of his giving, the journal would give to him. That following Christmas season, he had found the love of his life. It has followed those connected to that love ever since. Guiding them, nudging them. Revealing nothing directly but always pointing them toward the heart that was meant to connect with theirs."

"And now," Amada turned and grinned warmly at me, "it has made its way through the circle."

My stomach flipped like it was doing gymnastics and my gaze connected with Rashaad's. He was already looking at me, staring like he wanted to grab me and run off in the nearest sunset. I looked away, still not used to the intensity of his gaze.

Amada's voice grew tender. "Love finds us in many forms. Sometimes it's gentle, sometimes it's inconvenient. Sometimes, we pretend like it's not there because we aren't ready to face it."

Everyone laughed.

"And sometimes," she finished, "it waits until the moment we stop running from it. I am so happy that my granddaughter and her beautiful friends have decided to stop running from it." She raised her glass while everyone else in the room followed suit.

"Here's to no longer running. May the love that catches you, be worth the wait."

"Cheers!" everyone called out. Movement next to me caused me to turn. Just in time to see Rashaad slide into the empty seat next to me.

"Pickles." He deadpanned.

"Wall-E," I replied.

Before he could say anything else, Elodie stood up to thank everyone, and the room's attention shifted. But I could still feel Rashaad's warmth beside me like a gravitational pull.

Then, softly, just for me, he leaned in and said:

"I'm glad we stopped running."

My heart stopped and I turned to him, a smile pulling at my lips.

"Me too."

11

Deja

The reception had finally slowed into that soft, hazy after-glow part of the night; shoes discarded, makeup smudged, and everybody sweaty and full of enough alcohol to profess lifelong friendship to strangers. Elodie and Mekhi were still on the dance floor, swaying and singing the lyrics to Beyonce's 1+1 to each other like a slow-motion fairytale.

Brina tapped her glass with her fork. "Ladies," she announced dramatically, "assemble."

I laughed and followed her to the corner of the room where Audrey and Monae already sat in chairs in a half-circle, panting like they had just run around the room. They looked exhausted and blissful and just drunk enough to be honest. The journal sat on the small table in the center of the circle. It was closed now and empty, my story had already erased from its pages.

Brina plopped down beside me with a sigh. "Lord, I love weddings but why do they require so much walking? Nobody warns you about the cardio."

"Girl," Audrey snorted, "your heels are six inches tall. You did that to yourself."

"The price of beauty."

Monae crossed her legs, smiling at us like she was memorizing the moment. "We did it. All five of us."

I swallowed hard and for a moment, reality settled onto my shoulders. This wasn't just the end of the night. It was the end of something big. Something magical. Elodie finally joined us, breathless and happier than I'd ever seen her. Her wedding dress bunched in her arms so she could walk freely. She settled down next to me and slipped the veil off her head. "Grandmada says that the journal has one last thing to say."

We all looked at it, waiting for the familiar rustling and page flipping that we'd all come to know and love. Nothing happened. Elodie reached out, lifted the cover, and revealed a single sentence that hadn't been there earlier.

I leaned forward and read it out loud.

Real love is not found, it is chosen, again and again, in moments small and grand. Magic can open the door, but only courage can walk through it.

My throat tightened. "Well. That's rude," I said, blinking fast. "Making me cry in front of company like this."

Brina wiped her eyes. "It's true, though. Somehow that journal knew exactly what each of us needed."

Audrey nodded. "And exactly when we needed it."

Monae gave a crooked little smile. "Sometimes it shoved us. Sometimes it whispered. But it always pushed us toward the thing we were too scared to want."

Elodie closed the journal gently, like she was tucking a child into bed. "I think this is the end of its journey with us."

"So, what happens now?" I asked. "Do we bury it? Burn it? Mail it back to Santa?"

Audrey laughed. "Please don't subject those poor postal workers to this chaos."

"I think I'm supposed to keep it. Until it tells me who to give it to next." Elodie said. "One day, it's going to find someone else."

"I don't think it was all the journal." Monae whispered. "We are also a little magical, in our own right."

We all got quiet because we knew what she meant. The magic wasn't just the journal. It was also us. Our friendship, our growth, and the way we held each other through heartbreak, through fear, and through falling in love when it felt like jumping out of an airplane with no parachute.

I looked around the tiny circle. Four women who changed my life without trying. Women who saw all of my sharp edges and didn't flinch. Women who loved me as I learned to love myself.

"I guess this is the end," I said softly.

Elodie bumped my shoulder with hers. "Of the journal's story, maybe."

Brina grinned. "But not ours. Baby, we just getting started."

Audrey lifted her glass. "To real love," she said. "The kind you choose."

"And to us," I added. "The women who walked through every door the magic opened."

We clinked glasses. We drank and we held each other a little too long while the guests started leaving. And just like that, the journal closed; but the story, our story, keeps going.

The End...

Acknowledgments

Whew, I really did that! What started as a "wouldn't this be cute?" idea turned into a five-book Christmas series, and somehow, I lived to tell the tale. Writing one book is a lot. Writing five in a row? Unhinged behavior. But I made a promise, and keeping it mattered more than fear, doubt, or the many moments I considered deleting everything and pretending it never happened instead.

A Novel-Tea Christmas is officially complete, and my binge-watching heart hopes you'll binge-read it the same way. Snacks and copious amounts of hot chocolate are heavily encouraged. Huge thank you to my editor, Tylee Hardman, who swooped in during my panic era with the second book and never let me spiral alone. I remember sitting in the drive-thru line, discouraged after my first editor fell through, trying to tell myself that this wasn't a dumb idea to begin with, and then your developmental notes came in. You took a minute to pour life into me and my story before getting to work and that quick moment of encouragement settled deep in my soul. We are locked in now.

To my husband and best friend, Jared—cover designer, plot therapist, and professional "you've got this" guy—thank you for steadying my anxious brain and loving me through every chapter. Those moments in the living room, creating stories and bouncing ideas off each other mean more to me than I am able to verbalize. I love you.

To my girls, especially Tamara, Emily, and Jessica: thank you for hyping every release, listening to my rambling ideas, and holding me up when I didn't realize I needed it. When I'm rich, I'm buying each of you a car lol.

And to every reader, present and future: thank you for choosing my books, adding them to your TBR, and showing up for my stories. Sharing my work is terrifying, but you make it feel worth it every single time.

About The Author

Lauren Roach is a dog obsessed, true-crime loving, self-proclaimed book nerd that has always dreamed of becoming a published author. While most kids were frolicking in the sun, Lauren chose the path less sweaty and opted for the cool embrace of air conditioning while immersed in a book or busily penning fan fictions about whatever heartthrob boy band was on her radar.

Lauren's literary ambitions took a brief hiatus when she decided to venture into the world of criminal justice, earning both a bachelor's and a master's degree in the field. Even though she has yet to use either one of her degrees for anything career-related, she hopes to maybe use her criminal justice knowledge to one day write a really good mystery plot.

Fast forward to today, Lauren is happily residing in North Carolina with her lovely husband where she records episodes for her book centered podcast Lauren's Library and isn't afraid to break out a book in the middle of a social gathering. You can follow her work at

Instagram & Threads: @thebookybabe_
Tik Tok: @thebookybabe
Podcast: Lauren's Library Podcast
Website: www.sunflowerrosepublishing.com